CALUMET CITY
W9-CAL-148
3 1613 00399 0333

DATE DUE

Nothing with Strings

NPR's Beloved Holiday Stories

BAILEY WHITE

Scribner

New York London Toronto Sydney

CALUMET CITY PUBLIC LIBRARY

SCRIBNER
A Division of Simon & Schuster, Inc.
1230 Avenue of the Americas
New York, NY 10020

Copyright © 2008 by Bailey White

This book is a work of fiction. Names, characters, places, and incidents either are products of the author's imagination or are used fictitiously. Any resemblance to actual events or locales or persons, living or dead, is entirely coincidental.

All rights reserved, including the right to reproduce this book or portions thereof in any form whatsoever. For information address Scribner Subsidiary Rights Department, 1230 Avenue of the Americas, New York, NY 10020.

First Scribner hardcover edition October 2008

SCRIBNER and design are registered trademarks of The Gale Group, Inc., used under license by Simon & Schuster, Inc., the publisher of this work.

For information about special discounts for bulk purchases, please contact Simon & Schuster Special Sales at 1-800-456-6798 or business@simonandschuster.com.

Designed by Kyoko Watanabe
Text set in Legacy Serif

Manufactured in the United States of America

1 3 5 7 9 10 8 6 4 2

Library of Congress Cataloging-in-Publication Data is available.

ISBN-13: 978-1-4391-0226-8
ISBN-10: 1-4391-0226-0

IC
WHI

For Linda

01-10 24.00 ING

STORIES

Nothing with Strings

Meals-On-Wheels

IDA DIDN'T KNOW what to do in late September when the morning glories began taking over the living room. She had first noticed it in early July, just a little tendril nosing in between the screen and the window frame, but now a thicket of morning glories trailed along the picture molding and swagged down over the windows. "Heavenly Blue," but the blossoms faded to a kind of purple and left exotic violet smears wherever they fell.

"Why don't you just cut them off at the window and drag the vines away?" said the Meals-On-Wheels girl. "This purple will never wash out of your slipcovers."

The Meals-On-Wheels girl irritated Ida sometimes with these thorough and practical suggestions. "Why don't you just . . ." with the *just* implying that it would be the simplest thing in the world for any person of even the most meager intelligence, and only an old fool would not know what to do when Heavenly Blue morning glories came into the house and stained the furniture purple.

"Cut them off at the window," Ida said to herself, and she actually did stand by the window for just a minute with a pair of big orange-handled scissors. It was nighttime, and there were no open blooms, just the drooping, spent ones from that morning already turning purple at the edges. But then the telephone rang. It was Judy, saying, "How was your day?" just like she always did. All Judy really wanted to know was if Ida was still alive and well enough to answer the telephone. There was always a sigh of relief from California after Ida's hello, and the "How was your day?" was just extra talk really.

"Everything is fine," Ida said, then she told a little story about Mr. Rice down at the birdseed store, so Judy could hear that her mind was still sharp and her speech not slurred. When they finally said good-bye and Ida went back into the living room, she noticed tomorrow's fat, spiraling buds, and she put the scissors back in the drawer and went to bed.

In the morning Richard Nixon was in the kitchen again, scrambling eggs and then scrubbing out the frying pan with Dawn dishwashing liquid. He had ruined three frying pans so far. Ida lay in bed looking up at the white ceiling. There wasn't anything she could do about these thoughts after all, but just think them and let them go on. By the time she washed her face and put on her dress and went into the kitchen, she had it straight. There were her frying pans hanging on their hooks, and everything was just as she had left it the night before. It was only that Richard Nixon dream again, she told herself.

✦

That afternoon there was a new Meals-On-Wheels girl. The first thing about her was, she didn't come to the back porch and bang the screen door and bellow out, "Meals-On-Wheels!" This new girl knocked on the front door, and when Ida opened it, she didn't come bustling in, clutching the styrofoam tray against her bosom. Instead, she just stood in the doorway gazing at the morning glories.

"Now that is the prettiest thing I have ever seen in my life," she said, and right then Ida realized why she had not been able to just cut the vines off at the window and drag them out.

The new Meals-On-Wheels girl didn't just set the styrofoam tray down on the kitchen table and arrange the plastic spoon and fork and paper napkin with little twitchy, snatchy movements, then flounce out with a "Have a nice day!" The new Meals-On-Wheels girl got one of Ida's good plates out of the dining room cupboard and rummaged around in drawers until she found a proper spoon and fork. "You shouldn't have to eat off plastic," she said. Ida had to wash the dishes after she ate, but she didn't mind. It was nice to see her grandmother's old Flight and Barr Worcester again. The new Meals-On-Wheels girl had reached it right down off a high shelf.

The next day the new Meals-On-Wheels girl brought Ida a little iced cake she had made herself. "Just because you're old, that doesn't mean you should have to eat this goop," she said, and she threw the Meals-On-Wheels Jell-O into the garbage. She stepped on the little lever so hard that the lid flew up and then popped shut with such a snap that Ida grinned and said, "Ha!"

The Meals-On-Wheels girl dished up the rice, meat loaf, and beans on yesterday's plate and got a dessert plate from the china cabinet for the little cake. Then she sat down and crossed her arms on the table and watched Ida eat.

"I'm a good cook," the girl said. "I used to cook for

prisoners. 'Just because you shot a clerk at a Jiffy food store for a six-pack of beer, that doesn't mean you should have to eat instant mashed potatoes for the rest of your life,' I used to tell them."

Ida stopped with the fork halfway to her lips.

"I used to bake little cakes for them. Each prisoner got his own individual cake. I put a different flower on every single cake—red, yellow, blue; green leaves. I have a pastry tube."

◆

"She used to make little cakes for prisoners," Ida told Judy that night.

"That's nice, Mama," said Judy.

"She has a pastry tube."

"She sounds like a nice little friend for you, Mama."

◆

"Sex," said the Meals-On-Wheels girl. She was ironing one of Ida's linen napkins. "I gave it up." She pressed the napkin from the back, against a folded tea towel, so the corded letters *ICW* would stand up high. "I just lost interest in it. Turned forty, that was it. Poof. Gone. Elvis has left the building."

"Oh," said Ida.

"I don't miss it though. Now I have more energy for other things. My mind is freed up." The girl folded the napkin in threes with the raised letters in the center, poured jasmine tea into Ida's blue-and-white teacup, and put three little biscuits on a dish. "Devonshire scones," she said. "They're flavored with rose water."

Ida had forgotten how beautiful good tea looked in a fine cup, the gold against the white. She took a sip, then she said boldly, "Sometimes your mind can be too free."

"Yeah?"

"Yes. Sometimes your mind might tell you that Richard Nixon is in the kitchen cooking eggs late at night." Ida had never told anyone about Richard Nixon; they had put her old friend Louise into Shady Rest Nursing Home after she told her niece that John James Audubon was living in her attic, and it had been all downhill from there.

But the Meals-On-Wheels girl didn't even flinch. "Fried or scrambled?" she said.

"Well," said Ida, nibbling on a scone, "they were scrambled eggs."

The Meals-On-Wheels girl said, "You couldn't pay me to eat an egg cooked by Richard Nixon!"

Ida smiled and the Meals-On-Wheels girl smiled back. The whole room smelled like a flower garden.

The next morning Ida noticed that the Heavenly Blue morning glories had made the long span from the last living-room window, and a little slip of vine was balanced on the top of the bedroom-door molding, reaching for the light. She got out of bed and put on her slippers, but instead of creeping down the hall clutching her bathrobe at her neck and peeking around corners, Ida marched right into the middle of the kitchen with her arms crossed and said in a strong voice, "You couldn't pay me to eat an egg cooked by Richard Nixon!"

◆

"Do you know any old songs?" asked the Meals-On-Wheels girl. "I play clawhammer banjo, bump-ditty strum," and she did a pretty little dance across the porch. "'I Wish I Was a Mole in the Ground'? 'Pig in a Pen'? 'Praise God I'm Satisfied'?"

"I used to know 'Once I Courted a Waxful Maid,'" said Ida.

"And?"

Ida hesitated, rocking in the rocking chair for a while, then she said, "'With dark and roving eye.'"

"Whoo, baby! Keep going."

"My daughter, Judy, hates those songs because the

women always end up beat to death or stabbed in the heart."

"Judy! What does she know?" The Meals-On-Wheels girl sat down on the swing with a pad and a pencil. "Sing me the whole thing."

✦

"I just think you'd enjoy your afternoons more over at the senior center, Mama," Judy said that night. "A trained staff, planned activities, little craft projects to make you feel useful—"

"'And deep into her bosom he plunged the fatal knife,'" sang Ida. "I just remembered! 'Way down in lone green valley.'"

"—crocheting baby booties for newborns," said Judy.

But Ida wanted to get off the phone so she could write it all down for the Meals-On-Wheels girl before she forgot.

✦

"Look at all this nice stuff," said the Meals-On-Wheels girl, looking into the hall cupboards. "It's a shame the way this silver is all tarnished, and this linen yellowing along the folds."

"It's my arthritis," said Ida. "I can't do all that rubbing."

"What good is that daughter of yours out in California?" The Meals-On-Wheels girl took down the silver pitcher and turned it in her hands. "Look at this pretty thing, it's plumb black."

"She calls me up on the long-distance telephone every night."

"To see if you're live or dead, that's all she wants to know. I bet she doesn't even come Thanksgiving."

"Well, she has her family."

But the Meals-On-Wheels girl was rummaging under the kitchen sink for the silver polish and a rag. "You sit down and keep me company while I work. Talk to me, sing me some songs."

It had been a long time since Ida had kept anybody company. It felt good to sit and talk about just anything at all. "My neighbor Louise thought John James Audubon was living in her attic," she said. "That's why they took her off to Shady Rest."

"John James Audubon was a born liar," said the Meals-On-Wheels girl. "He never told the truth once in his whole life. I wouldn't want a man like that living in my attic. You couldn't count on him."

"That's exactly what Louise said. He would talk all night, trying to get her to go up there with him and all those dead birds. But when anybody else came, he wouldn't say a word."

"He'd lay low then, wouldn't he?"

"Louise told them, 'Go on up there, you'll see him.' And they did, but all they saw was a dead chimney swift, so they took her off to Shady Rest."

"The lying dog," said the Meals-On-Wheels girl.

At the end of the afternoon all the forks and spoons were polished and gleaming in their rosewood box, and the Meals-On-Wheels girl left with a basket full of linen to wash with Clorox. "I'll bring it back and iron it tomorrow and we'll sing. I love to sing when I iron."

◆

"How was your day?" said Judy that night, and Ida said, "Everything is fine."

◆

By early November the Meals-On-Wheels girl had polished all the silver and washed all the dishes from way in the backs of cupboards and closets, and laundered and ironed all the tablecloths, napkins, and piles of useless little lacy things, heavy with embroidery.

"I'm going to start in on you next," she told Ida.

She took out a tape and measured Ida around the waist and down the back from the neck to the knee. "Bet you didn't know I could sew. What's your favorite color?"

"It's blue," said Ida.

"Heavenly blue, I should have known that." The Meals-On-Wheels girl held one of the morning glories up to Ida's cheek. With the cooler weather they were putting on their last lavish display of bloom, and all the windows were draped with garlands of flowers.

✦

"Everything is fine," Ida told Judy. "The Meals-On-Wheels girl is making me a blue dress for Thanksgiving. We're going to have a picnic in the park."

✦

Thanksgiving was a perfect fall day, bright, cool, and windy. "Come look," said the Meals-On-Wheels girl, opening up a white box on Ida's bed. Heavenly blue—the dress was exactly that color, as if the Meals-On-Wheels girl had tucked and pleated several yards of October sky. It was lined with white like the throats of the morning glories, with a shiny silver band sewed into the insides of pleats and folds, so that silver flashed from hidden places. The Meals-On-Wheels girl held it up high and put it on over Ida's head. "I made it like an eleven-o'clock morning glory."

Ida could see that the fabric relaxed into graceful folds, like a morning glory right before noon, when it just begins to droop. "It's the most beautiful dress I've ever seen," she said.

"You're right about that. I worked my fingers to the bone on that thing." The Meals-On-Wheels girl stood back, turned Ida around and around, then clapped her hands and laughed out loud. "Now come with me to Paradise," she said.

It was nothing but Paradise Park, Ida knew that, just a grove of pine trees on the edge of downtown. But they went all the way along the azalea path to the Nat Williams Memorial Daffodil Garden in the middle of the park.

On the slate table the Meals-On-Wheels girl had spread Ida's grandmother's damask tablecloth with the embroidered crest and the *ICW.* The table was set with the panel Dresden china Ida hadn't seen in years and the repoussé silver. There was the newly polished water pitcher, the wineglasses with the gold rims, and the silver epergne, with morning-glory leaves trailing along its branches.

"Look at us," said the Meals-On-Wheels girl. "Aren't we pretty?" They sat down on the concrete bench and drank glasses of wine while the Meals-On-Wheels girl played "Swannanoa Tunnel," "In the Shadow of the Pines," and "The Mermaid Song" on the banjo. After that, Ida couldn't keep up with all that went on. There was laughing and talking and the rosy light filtering through the dogwood leaves, and for no reason at all Ida began reciting the names of old daffodils—Butter and Eggs, Hoop-Petticoat, Campernelle, and Pheasant's Eye. Then there was a different kind of wine, and suddenly they were eating a clear golden soup with little green lemony bits floating on top in the silver consommé dishes, and the Meals-On-Wheels girl sang out, "All the flavor is in the feet!" After that, food seemed to appear out of nowhere—snowy mashed potatoes, little green onions, crackling bread, and greasy collards. Everything that should have been hot was hot, and everything that should have been cold was cold. At one point between the creamed Jerusalem artichokes and the caramel custard, Ida and the Meals-On-Wheels girl held hands and danced around the liriope border, singing "Way Down in Lone Green Valley." The Meals-On-Wheels girl's long red skirt twirled around her ankles, and she swayed and bowed and pranced out her little feet over the dormant daffodils.

Ida woke up in the morning with the feeling that she had grit under her eyelids. Her feet were cold, and she lay in bed for a long time, staring at the ceiling. But before she had time to think, she heard, "Meals-On-Wheels!" bellowed out from the back porch, then heavy walking, and suddenly there was the old Meals-On-Wheels girl standing in the bedroom door.

"I'm back!" she said, then made a slow turn with her hands on her hips. "Now you've got you a mess. And don't be asking me to go at it with the 409 and a rag; you're going to have to get the professionals in here for this."

Slowly Ida pushed back the covers and put her feet on the floor. It had turned cold in the night, the first freeze. All along the walls the dead morning glories hung, festooning the windows in slimy tatters, and smearing the woodwork and windowpanes.

"But," said Ida, "what about . . . where is . . ." But the old Meals-On-Wheels girl was already back in the kitchen laying out the styrofoam tray and the plastic fork and spoon and talking about surgery.

"There I was, cut open from here to here, and them telling me to get up and walk up and down that hall within twenty-four hours. I was hanging on to them railings, I can tell you that. They said two months, it's been two months, I'm dragging, but I'm here; now get on up, honey, you need to eat you something, I got to get over to Miss Eunice."

"But what about my little friend," said Ida, teetering in the kitchen doorway in her slippers, "who made cakes for prisoners, a different flower on each cake, with little leaves—"

The Meals-On-Wheels girl stopped and looked hard at Ida. "Honey? You all right?"

"That other Meals-On-Wheels girl, the one whose mind was freed up; she had energy for other things."

"Honey, there was nobody but me, and then Richard and Albert each took half my route when I was out, and now I'm back. Listen, I'm going to get Doris to come see about you. Where's my list? What was that daughter's name out in California—Judy, what was it? *A*-something."

"Auerbach," said Ida, creeping down to the hall cupboards. "Come look," she said to the Meals-On-Wheels girl. "She washed all the linens, she polished the silver, we danced on the daffodils and sang 'Where Roses Bloom and Fade' and drank soup flavored with chicken feet. You'll see." Ida opened the cupboard doors.

But instead of neat stacks of linen tablecloths and napkins smelling of Clorox and sunshine, there was nothing but a square of white shelf paper slid crooked, with one corner folded up against the back wall. "Here," said Ida, opening up the china cabinet. But there was no silver pitcher, no Royal Crown Derby tea set, no Flight and Barr Worcester, no rosewood box—just air, smelling slightly of camphor.

From the kitchen Ida could hear the Meals-On-Wheels girl talking on the telephone.

"You might be wanting to think about another level of care. . . .

"I'll get Doris from over at Shady Rest, if you've done the paperwork. . . .

"Yeah, but she's got a mess here in the house now, some kind of plant died on the walls."

Then Ida began remembering flashes of things: the gold thread in the Meals-On-Wheels girl's swirling red skirt, the red wine in the gold-rimmed glasses, the glowing dogwood leaves, the dew on the silver pitcher, and the glint of silver from the heavenly blue dress.

"Yeah, she's talking good, but she's not making much sense. Here she is," said the old Meals-On-Wheels girl, and she handed Ida the telephone.

"Mama?" said Judy.

Ida smiled and said, "Everything is fine."

The Long Black Veil

EVER SINCE HER mother died of Alzheimer's disease a year ago, Charlene has been plagued by suitors. Charles from the furniture store, who came to deliver her new sofa and then didn't want to leave; Big Jim, who drops in to quote from the Bible about men and women; Larry from down the street, who comes over on his riding lawn mower and talks about Mars. These men are not skillful wooers. They remind Charlene of big, obsolete machinery—a cane grinder or cottonseed press.

"Now, if you got anything big you want moved, I can come back after work," says the furniture man.

"No," says Charlene, "everything is exactly where I want it, thank you."

"'And the Lord God said, It is not good that the man

should be alone; I will make an help meet for him. She shall be called Woman,'" says Big Jim. He stands there and stands there for so long that soon all Charlene can see are his new bleached-white teeth and his new white tennis shoes glowing in the dark.

In the morning Larry rides over on his riding mower and offers to cut her grass.

"I've got my own mower," says Charlene. But Larry won't go home. He makes himself comfortable on the seat of his lawn mower and goes on and on about Mars, how big and red it is.

"You know what?" he says, as if he's just thought of it. "We ought to walk down to the lake yard one night and look at Mars, just you and me."

"Thank you," says Charlene, "but I can see Mars from my own backyard."

After she saw that movie *The Bridges of Madison County,* Charlene used to think from time to time how nice it would be if a handsome stranger would come up in the yard one day, someone tall and distant, with a slow smile and a mysterious skill. But about the time that movie came out was when Charlene's mother first started to wander off. If Clint Eastwood himself had pulled up in the backyard in a pickup truck, she couldn't have driven off with him; her mother would have ended up at the bottom of Lake Despera.

Now her mother was dead and here were all these men, greasing up the old rusty gears of romance, wanting to move her furniture and show her Mars. But Charlene was not born yesterday. She knows she is the same little dumpy lady she was before her mother died and left her over $600,000. She knows all they want is to marry her so they can plop down on her new sofa and put their big white feet up on her coffee table and order off after that metal-flake bass boat and Evinrude motor they saw advertised on TV and put it on her debit card.

◆

"Tell them all to get lost," said Clarence down at the antique mall. "Tell them you don't need a man, thank you very much. Tell him to crank up that riding mower and shove off, buddy."

It was a drizzly Monday in early fall, and Charlene was out at Clarence's Antique Mall sitting in one of the cozy little rooms Clarence had created out of used furniture—a camel-backed sofa, two wing chairs, a lamp with a fringed shade, a worn-out rug on the concrete floor. Clarence was glad to have her. "People have no vision," he always said. "You have to show them everything. Just sit there. Look comfortable. You are demonstrating the purpose of furniture."

It was peaceful in the antique mall on this damp Monday. There were no customers, just the intoxicating fumes of neat's-foot oil and furniture wax, the soporific drone of the traffic on 90, and the little patter of rain on the metal roof. Charlene was just thinking how warm she was, how her back didn't hurt at all, and how she could almost go to sleep, and the next thing she knew her head snapped back and her eyes flew open. There was a little crash and a cry, "Jesus God!"

A man stepped back from the shards of a broken cup, staring wildly at Charlene. He sank down in the wing chair and put his head down.

"You scared me to death," he said. "I thought you were one of those plaster statues that look so real." He put a hand on Charlene's knee. His eyes were wide and wild. "I'm so sorry. I didn't know you were alive."

From all that peace and quiet, the cozy little room was suddenly a bustle of activity. There was Clarence with the broom and the dustpan, the man stood up and staggered back, not quite ready—and reached for his wallet. Charlene, in that confused state of people who have just woken up in a public place, wondered, Did I drool? Was my mouth hanging open? Embarrassed to look the man in the face, she watched his hands fumble out a wad of money from a pocket and slide off the rubber band. She saw the big old face of Ben Franklin, Ben

Franklin, Ben Franklin, flipping out from under his thumb, while Clarence held up both hands and said, "No, no, no, put your money away. It was just a piece of cheap blue transferware."

"Just let's all sit down for a minute," said Clarence. He brought a pot of tea and some little cookies. There was an awkward silence, just the rain on the roof and in the distance a police siren heading west.

"I'm sorry I scared you so bad," said Charlene. "I know that can startle a person, when you think things are one way and then you suddenly find out it's something entirely different."

"I'm just jumpy," said the man. "I'm trying to get to Pensacola. I haven't slept in a couple of days." He took a handful of Clarence's cookies. "I don't know if I'm sleepier or hungrier."

"What ails you?" said Charlene. "Why can't you sleep?"

The man munched and munched on his mouthful of cookies and closed his eyes. He lolled his head back and took a deep, ragged breath. "Oh," he said, and thought awhile. "I just miss Johnny Cash so bad, that's all."

"Well, you ought to go on home and get in the bed," said Charlene. "You need your sleep."

The man started to laugh and kept on laughing, not loud, just chuckling to himself with his eyes closed.

"Honey, I just can't do that," he said.

Clarence went over into another booth and started flipping through a box of records. He opened up the lid of an old record player, checked out the frayed cord, and picked a wad of dust off the needle. "I don't sell merchandise that doesn't work," he said.

There was a loud humming sound, then the *bump-bump-bump* as the needle went round and round, coming up on Johnny Cash at Folsom Prison, singing "Long Black Veil." A little scratch in the record almost kept the beat. The man sat back in the wing chair and smiled. Johnny Cash sang, "She stood in the crowd and she shed not a tear."

"That's so sad," said Charlene, "to think he would love a woman who would do him that way."

"Come on." The man shoved himself up out of the chair and took both Charlene's hands in his. "Dance with me."

It was so smooth and unexpected that Charlene could not think yes or no. She just all of a sudden found herself slow-dancing cheek to cheek with a total stranger to Johnny Cash singing "Long Black Veil."

At first he went pretty good, and Charlene could feel the music in the dancing, but toward the end of the song he had slowed down until he was almost standing still, and finally when Johnny Cash got them to the gallows he was just standing there, leaning on Charlene so heavily she felt if she stepped out from under him, he would fall right down. She led him stumbling backward into one of the antique mall's bedrooms and sat him down on a little four-poster bed.

"I just want to rest my eyes for a minute, just a little minute," he said, and next thing they knew he was sound asleep, breathing with a little rasping sound at the back of his throat.

There is something vulnerable about a sleeping person that brings out tender feelings of protection and care, not quite maternal. Charlene and Clarence looked at the man for a while, then went on about their business, each feeling the weight of that trust in his own way.

Charlene went home and thawed out a casserole and cooked a pot of rice and got her best tomato off the windowsill. Clarence put up the CLOSED sign on the door and turned off the outside lights and went back to work oiling a leather ottoman.

The man slept on and on. It got dark—the quiet early dark that comes to small towns on the eastern edge of a time zone. At six Charlene came back with her chicken divan and a pan of biscuits and a steamed pudding. Soon the smell of food took over the smell of furniture wax and neat's-foot oil.

The man woke up in an orderly way. First he stared

at the ceiling, then he sat up and stared at his feet. Then he looked all around the antique mall, and last he looked at Charlene and Clarence.

"I thought you might want to get you a little something to eat before you head on," said Charlene, "but Mamie's is closed Mondays, so I brought you some supper."

Clarence set up a little eating place at an enamel-topped table in a booth selling antique kitchen gadgets. "How about this old Buffalo china, now doesn't that look festive? Just don't tell Esther."

The man sat down gingerly. "What is this place? Is this some kind of a home?"

"Where have you been?" said Clarence. "You never saw an antique mall?"

Charlene piled up the plates with chicken divan and a slice of tomato for color. She felt a little shy, remembering the feel of the man's cheek on hers and his arms heavy around her waist as Johnny Cash sang "been in the arms of my best friend's wife." She put an extra slice of tomato on his plate and stole a glance at him. He was sitting very still with his hands in his lap staring right at her face.

"Are you an angel?" he asked.

Clarence laughed and said, "She *is* an angel." Charlene looked down and worried over her chicken divan. Was there too much salt? Too much curry? Was it cold in the middle? She took the first bite. No, it was perfect. She relaxed. Then it almost turned into a regular meal, three people eating together and visiting. Clarence explained the concept of an antique mall, the man explained that his car had broken down that afternoon, was in the shop, something in the transmission. "I can't make it to Biloxi tonight," he said.

"Did you leave it at Axelrod's?" asked Clarence. "Axelrod has a good transmission man."

"Yes, Axelrod's."

Charlene asked him did he have a place to stay, since the motel had closed down. "We're not exactly a big tourist destination up here in north Watson County," she said.

There was a silence, then Clarence said, "You can go on and stay here tonight. Just don't steal anything."

The man looked around. "You know, I don't see a thing in here I need." He took an eggbeater off the Peg-Board wall and spun its handle. *"Vroom!"* he said, and smiled at Charlene and winked, as if it were a little joke just between them.

✦

That night when Charlene got home, she had a happy, reckless feeling. She hummed "Long Black Veil" as she washed the dishes, and instead of weary and polite, she felt irritated and snappy when Larry showed up at the back door.

"I noticed you were gone a long time after dark and just got back," said Larry. "I just wanted to check on you, see if everything is all right."

"I've been out." Then she added, although it wasn't exactly the truth, "Dancing."

"Dancing! Well, Esther called me and said she saw the lights on down at the antique mall long after closing time, and rode by there and said she thought she saw you and Clarence in there eating in her kitchen booth. Said she thought she saw somebody else in there eating with y'all, she didn't recognize him."

Right then Esther drove up, and then Big Jim came over, and they all came up on Charlene's porch and stood there as if their feet had put down roots.

"What is Clarence thinking, having total strangers down there eating and drinking?" said Esther.

"Don't blame Clarence," said Charlene. "That was me. The poor man was hungry, and Mamie's was closed, so I took him a little something to eat."

"You sat down and ate with somebody you don't even know? A total stranger?" said Larry. "You cooked for him?"

"Well, he was hungry," said Charlene. "And sleepy,

so Clarence let him take a nap in that little four-poster bed." She didn't mention the broken cup or "The Long Black Veil" or the dancing. She didn't tell them that he had fallen asleep in her arms and called her an angel.

"What?" said Esther. "Clarence has got people eating and sleeping down at the antique mall! Might as well just shack up down there!"

Larry put his arm around Charlene's shoulder the way you would do a child and talked slowly and carefully to her as if she couldn't understand English. "Honey, you're so sweet, but you just can't do that. Why, he could have been a wanted criminal!"

"He could have been on drugs," said Big Jim. "Did you get a look at his pupils? Was they pinpoint or dilated?"

Shot a man in Reno, thought Charlene, *just to watch him die.* It was the second time that day a man had put an arm around her and called her honey, but how different it felt this time. Charlene twitched out from under Larry's arm. "He wasn't on drugs," she said. "He was just sleepy."

"I am going down there first thing in the morning and look at my dishes, and if there is a single chip—" said Esther.

"Wait!" said Larry. "What are we thinking?" He bumped his forehead with the heel of his hand. "He could be a terrorist! He could be gon' hijack one of those jets from Eglin Air Force Base and fly it up to New York City! Did he look foreign?"

"And I am going to call Mozelle and tell her Clarence is putting rank strangers to bed on that lovely ivory linen spread with the hand-tatted inserts," said Esther. "I may just have to pull out of that mall. There's more money down at the beach anyway."

"Well, what was he doing here?" said Big Jim. "Where was he going?"

"He was on his way to Pensacola," said Charlene.

After some disgruntled shuffling around on the porch, they all finally went down the steps and back home, mumbling and muttering, and Charlene was alone—just her and Mars, low and red in the sky behind her.

When Charlene finally got to bed, she could not sleep. She lay there and lay there, squirming and flapping the covers. She kept thinking about Larry's breath, smelling like coffee and cigarettes and peppermint, and Esther's snipey little face and her shrill, fast talk.

Let her take her tacky stuff to the beach! thought Charlene. Esther called it "collectible"; Clarence called it junk. Then Charlene thought about the stranger, at this very moment peacefully sleeping in the little four-poster bed. She hoped he wouldn't get cold, that the lights from 90 wouldn't shine in his eyes, that the train wouldn't wake him up when it came through at two thirty.

Charlene slept fitfully. In the middle of the night she woke up with a start, feeling that someone was watching her, someone with a big face and a little sly smile and hair curling to his shoulders. Benjamin Franklin's face was on a hundred-dollar bill, she remembered, and that wad of bills in the man's pocket must have been an inch thick. Her thoughts came one by one, not crowding, but each taking its turn. "Pensacola," he had said, but then later "Biloxi." "Yes," he had said to Clarence, "at Axelrod's, something in the transmission." But Axelrod's was closed Mondays, just like Mamie's.

Charlene put on her clothes and drove down to the antique mall. It had turned cold and a column of steam rose off Lake Despera and spread through the town, muffling the glow of the streetlights.

He was awake, too, prowling around in the antique mall like a cat. He let her in without a word. Charlene made up the little four-poster bed, smoothing Mozelle's linen bedspread tight and checking for snagged threads. She stacked Esther's dishes neatly. There were no chips. The man just stood by the door, watching and waiting.

"Come on," said Charlene. "Get in the car. I'm going to take care of you."

They drove west on 90, then turned north on 331, toward Alabama. "Fasten your seat belt," said Charlene. Once they got out of the reach of the mist of Lake Despera, it was a clear night, with the moon glowing on barn roofs and making shadows in the woods and silvering up the backs of Charolais cows in the fields.

What Would They Say in Birmingham?

IT ALL STARTED in the bathroom in the back of the bookstore in Florinna, Alabama, the store owner, Mrs. Horne, gesturing magnificently at the blank wall and talking about Arabian stallions, and the mural painter, Lucy, backed up against the toilet, nodding and saying, "Yes, yes," while wondering how in the world she could possibly paint seven horses in a race with the wind around the toilet-paper holder and faux-marble sink.

Lucy spent a lot of time painting in small rooms because of the idea people had that a mural "opened up the space." Before 2005 she had painted mostly coastal scenes in new developments along the beach, but Hurricane Katrina had taken the charm out of blue herons in low-lying marshes at dusk, and sunlit waves on gleaming sands. Now she found herself farther inland, painting alpine scenes, rushing brooks and country roads winding toward distant mountains.

Mrs. Horne, the bookstore owner, had decided on a Vermont village with a red barn and a church steeple, but last night she had gone to an inspiring neighborhood-development meeting where the speaker, a handsome man with a square jaw and penetrating eyes, had talked about a sense of place. "Build your own memories into this town!" he commanded. "Sure it's a beautiful old town with loads and loads of history. But it's your town now, and you must give it your own history. Your grandmother's porch, your great-aunt's garden, a scene from your favorite book. Build into the town everything that you love."

So Mrs. Horne threw out all Lucy's sketches of Peacham, Vermont, and decided she wanted for her mural a rendition of the frontispiece of her favorite book as a child, Wesley Dennis's magnificent illustration of seven Arabian stallions dashing across the desert in Marguerite Henry's book *King of the Wind.*

The town was the little old town of Florinna, Alabama. It had boomed when the Jackson Lumber Company established a mill there in 1895 and shipped out

2 million board feet of tongue-and-groove, end-matched rift flooring a day to cities in the Northeast and overseas to Europe. The optimistic, forward-looking settlers of Florinna built sturdy, straightforward heart-pine houses with long windows opening onto wide, sloping porches. They planted hundreds of baby live-oak trees all up and down the streets. They built a brick school on the hill, and one brick downtown street with everything anybody could possibly need or want: a feedstore, a grocery store, a drugstore, a hardware store, and a dry goods store. But in 1916 the planer mill burned, and in 1930 the Depression came, and in the 1960s the road just east of Florinna became an access road to I-10, and one by one the stores shut down, the porches sagged on the houses, the windows on the school were boarded up, and Florinna children were bused to the big, new school in the east end of the county. For forty years the only things that continued to thrive in Florinna were the live-oak trees and Smash Dykes's feedstore.

Then Hurricane Katrina hit, and the real estate developers turned their backs on the coast, took off their sunglasses, and saw for the first time, fifty miles inland and 120 feet above sea level, the peaceful, little old abandoned town of Florinna, with its oak-shaded brick streets and its Victorian downtown. "Whoa!" they said, and they started writing contracts. The hardware store became an art gallery selling folk art, the dry goods store became a gift shop belching out the scent of Yankee candles, and the grocery store had a sushi bar. Big tubs of geraniums lined the sidewalks, a vacant lot was turned into a pocket park, and now after just one year Florinna was hovering on the edge of cute.

Mrs. Horne, fresh from her divorce with nothing but her white cat, Precious, under her arm and $3 million in her bank account, came down from Birmingham and set up her book and gift store in the old drugstore building right next to Smash Dykes's feedstore. She called it White Cat Books.

"First I thought of cats for the mural," Mrs. Horne said to Lucy, "a whole wall of cats."

From the front of the store Lucy heard *knock-knock-knock.* "Do I hear—"

"But then I thought, no, no, no, this is a bookstore, it needs to be a scene from a famous book, and I thought of *Lad: A Dog,* but nobody reads *Lad: A Dog* anymore, everybody's into shar-peis—I'm an animal lover, Lucy, I bet you were beginning to guess that."

"Yes," said Lucy. "Is somebody—"

"And then last night Pierre Lepont said, 'Build in your own memories, this is *your* town.' That was a pivotal moment for me, Lucy, because this *is* my town." Mrs. Horne raised her arms dramatically, as wide as she could in the small space, and hugged herself with her eyes closed. "It's my town, and it's my life, all my very own!"

"Is somebody knocking?" said Lucy.

Then they heard footsteps, and there was Smash Dykes standing in the doorway of the bathroom holding a white cat by the scruff of the neck.

"Ma'am," he said.

"Precious!" squealed Mrs. Horne. The cat dangled limp-wristed, with its tail curled under its belly and one eye pulled into a squint and its mouth pulled into a long smile. It looked at them peacefully through slitted eyes, as if in a meditative trance, and Mrs. Horne gathered it up, rump first, and cuddled it under her chin, gently swaying from side to side.

"My name is Smash Dykes, ma'am."

Smash Dykes looked like a combination of Cool Hand Luke and Moses from a bad movie of the Old Testament. He had those blue eyes and that regal nose, and a kind of still dignity to his face, caused by badly patched-up skin-cancer surgeries. He was the only person left in Florinna who was *from* Florinna, and he ran Dykes's Feed and Seed, the store his grandfather Lucien Dykes had opened in 1895. The store had crept along selling seed corn and crowder peas and fertilizer and grain to farmers in the county, but the developers of the new Florinna had set up a model farm on the outskirts of town, just for looks, with a white-painted fence and a wrought-iron gate and a bronze statue of a horse on a stone pedestal, with its head high and mane and tail flying. There were riding horses in the pasture, and a pair of Belgians to pull a wagon on parade days, and a herd of belted Galloway cows. The brand-new barn looked as if it came right out of *Charlotte's Web.*

Smash Dykes himself had been turned into a kind of pet, and in the old bead-board hoppers in Dykes's Feed and Seed he now kept fancy sweet feed and oats and organic chicken feed with no added antibiotics, where there used to be moldy scratch feed and laying mash.

Everybody loved Smash Dykes. The urban theorists said that he gave authenticity to the town, and the real estate developers called him Smash and winked and said that he was a real gentleman of the old school. They wrote up Smash Dykes and his family feedstore in their promotional literature and asked him to pose for photographs for their brochures. They shook their heads when Smash Dykes showed up for the photograph session dressed in a suit and tie, with his shoes shined and his hair parted and combed down with water. They gave him a gingham shirt and faded blue jeans and a pair of worn work boots and tried to get him to slouch. They loved the questions he asked at the charettes: "Now how are them cows gon' get to water, you got the creek fenced off." Joggers began to drop in at Dykes's Feed and Seed to shoot the breeze with Smash Dykes, leaning up against the grain bins in their nylon pants with zippers at the ankles. "Smash," they asked, "what do you think of this, and what do you think of that," just to hear him talk, and just for the satisfaction of being able to say, "Well, I had a nice visit with old Smash this morning."

Smash Dykes came to be the symbol of everything the ad brochures claimed about the New Florinna—authenticity, old-fashioned charm, the simple life, traditional rural values. Ladies living in the fixed-up old houses along the river had fancy chicken pens built in their backyards and were thrilled to gather their own eggs, and to consult with Smash Dykes about their flocks. They brought little ailing chicks in to him, cuddled in the palms of their hands.

"Ma'am, that biddy's got the gummy tail, ain't nothing you can do about it but snatch its head off," said Smash Dykes.

Then they would go home and talk about Smash Dykes among themselves and laugh about his "tough love."

Even Mrs. Horne's white cat, Precious, loved Smash Dykes, and instead of lolling on a satin pillow in the store window under the curlicue sign WHITE CAT BOOKS as Mrs. Horne had planned, he took to pacing back and forth in front of the door, meowing plaintively with his longing to get out of White Cat Books and dash over to Dykes's Feed and Seed.

One day when Smash Dykes brought Precious back to the bookstore, Mrs. Horne took him into the bathroom to see Lucy's mural. Lucy had the wall primed, and the beginnings of the background shaded in. Lucy showed Smash Dykes her preliminary sketches of the seven Arabian horses racing across the desert.

"Look like they got a little bit of quarter horse in them," said Smash Dykes. "You got that just right, how he's got them hind legs gathered up underneath him. You draw a mighty fine horse, ma'am."

"Thank you, Mr. Dykes," said Lucy.

"Smash," said Mrs. Horne, "I have a thing about horses, and I think there have been horses in your past. When I look at you, I see horses."

"Yes'm," said Smash Dykes. "I have had a right smart of dealing with horses in my time, and there was some good and some bad about it."

"I would love to hear your stories, Smash," said Mrs. Horne, and she led Smash Dykes out into the little sitting-room part of the bookstore, where she had reading lamps and comfortable furniture. "I bet you could tell the most fascinating horse stories, better than the stories in the books I sell."

"Yes'm, I could tell some horse stories'd make you want to just put your head in your hands and cry like a baby."

"You know," said Mrs. Horne, "when I was a little girl, my daddy bought me a horse, just the laziest, good-for-nothingest horse you ever saw. All he did was stand around half-asleep, with his bottom lip hanging down, but I loved him so, and I named him Trigger. Oh, I had such horse dreams, Smash!"

Mrs. Horne's favorite colors were lavender and pale green, and she was skillful with her clothes and makeup. She had soft blond hair and she smelled like heliotrope. Mrs. Horne sat down in the chair across from Smash Dykes, crossed her legs, and smoothed her skirt around her knees. She had pretty little hands and feet and she arranged them just so. "You know," she said, "I still dream of horses, but not of horses like my old Trigger. Oh, no! I dream of horses like the Arabian stallions in Lucy's painting, horses from books I've read, spirited horses with fire in their eyes and their heads and tails held high."

Smash Dykes didn't say a word, but sat there thoughtfully for a long time, while Precious meowed and gazed up at him.

By that afternoon Lucy had finished the background of the mural and begun to block in the horses. She was washing out her brushes when Mrs. Horne came in to admire the work and chat.

"You know," Mrs. Horne said, "I do believe Smash Dykes is a little sweet on me. Isn't that the cutest thing? The poor man was absolutely tongue-tied!"

"Or maybe he just didn't have anything to say," said Lucy.

"The silent type!" Mrs. Horne wagged a finger. "Still waters run deep!"

After that, Smash Dykes began showing up nearly every day at the bookstore, to see the progress of the mural and to sit in the comfortable reading lounge with Mrs. Horne. She fed him sesame wafers from the coffee shop—"I feel just like a little birdie, eating all these seeds," said Smash Dykes—and made him cups of green tea—"Tastes about like branch water," said Smash Dykes.

One day about a week into it, Mrs. Horne confided to him that she wasn't happy with the progress of the mural. "I feel so bad, Lucy has worked so hard, but there's something troubling about it," she whispered, leaning into Smash Dykes.

"Ain't nothing wrong with them horses, now," said Smash Dykes.

"It's not the horses, it's the background. It looks like something out of Desert Storm. Will you come with me when I confront her, Smash? I must be brave, but for this I need a man by my side."

"I'll be that man. Happy to."

Smash Dykes stood in the doorway as Mrs. Horne began, "We love the horses, Lucy, but there's something harsh about the background."

Lucy stood with her brush held lightly in her fingers, looking at the rock she had just painted. Those shadows had not been easy.

"Could you just put a tree or two in there?" said Mrs. Horne. "Not necessarily a *tree* tree, but just a suggestion of trees. I think it needs the softness of trees. What do you think, Smash?"

"I like trees," said Smash Dykes. "This whole town was built on the longleaf pine."

So Lucy worked another day and a half, wishing she got paid by the hour instead of the job, painting out rocks and painting in trees, and at last it was done.

"I love it, Lucy, I absolutely love it," said Mrs. Horne. "That is exactly what it needed, just that little touch of green." She signed the check and hung a roll of toilet paper under the thundering hooves of the bay horse. She stood back and clasped her hands delightedly under her chin. "Just in time for the parade!"

Then it was the week of the festival, and the whole town was scurrying to get ready for the first annual Florinna Fall Parade. Mrs. Horne hung banners and bunting all over White Cat Books and set up a display of the new Christmas books in the window. On Tuesday afternoon Mrs. Horne got Smash Dykes to drive her all the way to Dothan to get a truckload of potted chrysanthemums. It was after eleven by the time they got back and got all the plants unloaded, and it was one a.m. when Smash Dykes's truck pulled out of Mrs. Horne's driveway and headed slowly down the street with the headlights turned off.

The next day Mrs. Horne was all over town delivering pots of chrysanthemums, and whispering and giggling.

In the coffee shop, alternating pots of bronze and yellow: "You know how courtly he is! Why, it was just like something out of a book!"

At the gift shop, pinching off broken flower heads: "Alice, I'm telling you, he was down on his knees! I said, 'Smash, get up from there!'"

And to Lucy late in the afternoon: "Why, I had no idea what thoughts had been forming in that stony old head of his! It was one o'clock for heaven's sake, I was just exhausted, finally I just threw him out. I said, 'Smash, go home!' What in the world was he thinking?"

It was not a big day at Dykes's Feed and Seed. Smash

Dykes sold a ball of string and loaded fifty bales of hay for seats around a bonfire, but he didn't come out of the back of the store all day.

The next day was festival day, but long before daylight Lucy's telephone rang. It was Mrs. Horne, in a shrieking whisper: "Lucy! There is something in my yard! Lucy! Smash Dykes did this! What am I going to do? Lucy, please help me! Please just come over here. I'll pay you anything, I need help!"

Mrs. Horne met Lucy in the dark and led her through the dark house. "I can't turn on lights," she whispered. "No one can know about this. Look!" She threw open the back door. "Just look!"

There was a magnificent old crape-myrtle tree from the old Florinna days, its smooth trunks gleaming white, and a little row of Indian-hawthorn bushes Mrs. Horne had put in, and then right in the middle of the flower bed where the yard began to slope down to the river, something big and dark looked almost like a horse.

"What in the world . . . ," said Lucy.

It was a horse. It was the bronze horse from the entrance to the model farm, gleaming in the moonlight of Mrs. Horne's backyard, its head held high and its mane and tail flying, its majesty slightly impaired by a staggering tilt to the left where its supporting front leg had punched into the soft dirt of Mrs. Horne's Ophiopogon border.

"What was he thinking!" said Mrs. Horne.

"Why in the world . . ."

"Because I won't marry him!" shrieked Mrs. Horne. "The very idea! Give up that alimony check for a man who sells chicken feed and chews a mint-flavored toothpick! Me! I'm from Birmingham!"

"How did he get it off of there?" said Lucy. "How did he get it over here? It must weigh—"

"I don't care how he did it!" snapped Mrs. Horne. "We've got to get rid of it. Think about it, Lucy: Nothing can touch Smash Dykes. He is an iconic figure. But I'm just a little businesswoman! How will this make me look? I'm the one who will be ruined if this is found out." She paused and bravely choked back a sob. "What would they say in Birmingham?"

It was not hard to tip the horse over, with both of them pushing, and it shoved easily over the dewy Saint Augustine grass of Mrs. Horne's lawn and down the slope to the river. The head, tipped at that angle of arrogance, cut some gouges, but nothing that could not be sodded over. Once in the water, it wanted to float head down, with its pointy feet sticking up, and Lucy had to wade in waist deep and hold it down against the current while it filled with water from a hole in its belly. It rolled over on its side and floated high for a minute like a dead, bloated thing. With a *glug-glug-glug* sound, it sank lower and lower, and at last Lucy guided it out until she couldn't touch bottom anymore and gave it a shove. It caught on a snag, twirled once, and sank.

The first annual Florinna parade went on as scheduled, but it was a pitiful thing, with no enthusiasm. Nobody could think of anything but the missing statue. They all left the parade and went down to the gates of the farm and stood around, staring at all that was left of the bronze horse, its three feet on the stone pedestal, cruelly cut off at the fetlocks with a hacksaw. All they could talk about was who and why: vandals, college kids from Auburn, just for a lark, no understanding of values, what a shame, the first crime in our town. Nobody was thinking about the joys of the season, so Mrs. Horne turned out the lights on the display of Christmas books in the bookstore window and closed early. Everybody seemed to find Smash Dykes's feedstore a comforting place to be, and they congregated there and stayed until long after dark, drinking coffee and talking about the stolen statue. Smash Dykes didn't say much, just "Ain't it a shame" a few times. He sat in a straight chair by the woodstove, whittling a little horse out of basswood with his penknife, while Mrs. Horne's white cat wove in and out, rubbing up against his legs.

The Progress of Deglutition

IT WAS THANKSGIVING evening, that sweetly peaceful time after the dishes are washed and put away, and the turkey soup is simmering on the back of the stove, when Sally's husband, Dave, told her that their marriage felt like a snake around his neck, and he wanted a divorce.

It took Sally completely by surprise. She just sat there for a long time, staring at the first camellia in a glass dish on the dining room table, a White Emperor. Finally she said in a tiny, feeble voice, "What kind of snake?"

That sent Dave into a little raging fit. He stomped

around the living room, punching the upholstered furniture with his fist. "That's exactly what I mean!" he yelled at Sally in a high-pitched, angry voice. "I'm trying to tell you how I feel, I'm talking about my feelings, and all you want to know is 'What kind of snake?'"

It was all so fast and unexpected, Sally couldn't think or feel anything. Each breath she took seemed to leave a little empty space at the bottom of her lungs that she couldn't quite fill. She just sat there and said over and over, "Dave, Dave."

Finally Dave sat down on a side chair against the wall and without looking at Sally told the story of how he had been drinking a cup of coffee at the Java Hut when a young man walked by with a huge snake draped around his shoulders. The snake was so long he had to make two loops, and so heavy that you could see a droop in the young man, and a lag in his step. Then Dave started to cry. The thought had come to him all at once, he said, out of the blue: "That's exactly how I feel in my marriage."

All Sally could think of was the other times she had seen that same look of ragged desperation in Dave's eyes, and how she might comfort him. But when she reached out to him, he shrank back, and they just sat for a minute, staring at each other, miserable and helpless.

"I need time," Dave said. "I just need to be by myself,

to think things out. We'll decide what to do after the holidays."

✦

Sally's sister, Alice, met her at the door wearing a google-eyed, red-nosed reindeer sweater with her arms full of a bundle of blinking white lights. Through all the twinkling Sally could see the picturesque clutter of the beginnings of Christmas in the background: tissue-paper-lined boxes, heaps of greenery and red berries, Santa Claus, a gingerbread house, three papier-mâché wise men, and a hand-carved camel tipped over on its side. In the middle of it all her niece Lauren was lounging gracefully in a nest of bride magazines, staring with alarm at Sally, her eyes wide and her jaw dropped open, just like a nutcracker.

"Sally?" said Alice. "It's eleven thirty at night!"

"Let me in," said Sally. "Dave wants a divorce." And the next thing she knew she was drinking hot cider out of a Santa Claus mug and Alice was firing questions at her.

"Did you . . . ? Were there . . . ? How long . . . ?"

"No," said Sally, "no, no."

"Did you have a fight? Was there someone else?"

"No, no."

"Was there abuse—verbal abuse? Sally, did he hit you?"

"No," said Sally, "he only hit the sofa."

"Was there, have there been, had you been having"—Alice glanced furtively at Lauren—"personal difficulties of any kind?" On Alice's sweater, Rudolph's eyes wobbled with horror in their plastic sockets.

"No. Dave just said our marriage was cold, dead weight on his shoulders, like a snake."

"Oh, my darling!" Alice hugged Lauren protectively cheek to cheek. "You shouldn't be hearing these things! We all need to go to bed and think about this in the morning, when we're fresh."

Alice's guest room was perfectly designed for peaceful slumber, but Sally could not sleep. She lay down on the bed, stared at the ceiling, and counted up all the years she had been married to Dave. The first few fumbling years, setting up house together; then the years of comfortable routine; then those miserable two years when Dave quit his job at R & R Roofing to train bird dogs. They and all those dogs had had to live on her teacher's salary while Dave tried to make a go of it. But just as everybody had told him in the beginning, the plantations had their own dog men, and after two years Dave had to sell the dogs and crawl back to R & R with his tail between his legs, and nothing to show for it but the concrete-and-chain-link dog runs in the backyard filling up with leaves. That was when she had first seen that look in Dave's eyes she had seen tonight. But two years later Mr. Randolph retired, and they made Dave a partner at R & R. Then they had had Addie for those joyful four years, not knowing what was to come.

"Many marriages cannot survive the death of a child," the counselors had told them, but they had survived. It seemed as if the hard part must be over. What had gone wrong, and what should she have done about it?

Sally got up and sat in the fluffy chair by the window. She stared at the wall and thought about the first time she had ever seen Dave. He was putting a sheet-metal roof on the lunchroom of the school where she was a new teacher. His hair shone just like gold in the gleam from the roof, and he wore his nail apron slung low across his hips, the way Matt Dillon wore his holster in *Gunsmoke.*

The first time Dave ever spoke to her, Elvis Presley was singing "I Can't Help Falling in Love with You" on the jukebox at the Ship Ahoy. Dave looked over at her from the bar. "Howdy," he said. Sally had been embarrassed to look at him because she felt as if everybody in

3 1613 00399 0333

CALUMET CITY PUBLIC LIBRARY

the Ship Ahoy could surely tell Elvis Presley was singing that song just for her. It must show.

Sally drank all the water in the little pitcher by the bedside. It must have been a boa constrictor, she thought. She crept down the hall to the bathroom, then downstairs to the encyclopedias on the bottom shelf of the bookcase.

"All snakes are carnivorous and as a rule take living prey only," she read. "Many swallow their victims alive; others first kill it by smothering it between the coils of their body. The prey is always swallowed entire, and as its girth exceeds that of the snake, the progress of deglutition is very laborious and slow."

Sally went back upstairs and crawled into bed. Certainly their marriage wasn't the way it used to be, she thought. But was it supposed to be like that, after all this time? Wasn't there supposed to be a lag and a droop in a marriage after thirty-three years?

It was nearly six when she closed her eyes and remembered the turkey carcass she had left simmering on the back of the stove. Would Dave think to turn it off?

Then she was smelling coffee and hearing Alice and Lauren murmuring in the kitchen, the *ding-ding* of the timer and the drone of the dishwasher—all the little happy sounds of a modern household beginning to stir.

The Rudolph sweater was gone and Alice was wearing serious clothes this morning, a black linen sheath and a brown silk jacket. She poured coffee and said, "I've been thinking." She got the sugar bowl and the cream, and napkins. She sat down, then got back up and reached for saucers. "I've been thinking. If Dave is leaving you, then Dave should be the one to leave."

"But I'm the one with family," said Sally. "Dave doesn't have anywhere to go."

Alice glanced at Lauren, then jumped up and got three spoons. "This is such a busy time for us. It's the holiday season, and Bryan is coming in tomorrow, then the wedding in February. Christmas is a time for loving, happy, family feelings. You can't be feeling very happy right now, Sally—we've thought it might be easier for everybody if you stay with Aunt Ethel until you work things out."

◆

Aunt Ethel was an efficiency expert, famous for her rattrap histories and her lifelong "Total Time" records. She hated waste, sloth, and sloppiness. For Aunt Ethel, making a cup of coffee was an exercise in motion mindedness. Reach, grasp, use, return—there was not a wasted movement. With one hand she poured coffee into two cups and rinsed the pot, while with the other she opened a little pocket door in the wall and tossed the coffee grounds out onto the compost heap. With a gurgling sound the rinse water trickled out through a series of pipes and tubing onto a new bed of lettuces.

"Less than twenty-four hours ago I had a whole married life, with a husband and a house and a freezer full of food, and now all I do is sit in other people's kitchens and drink coffee," said Sally.

Aunt Ethel sat, a little, hard stump of a woman, gripping her coffee cup in both hands while Sally told it again, quicker this time: the peaceful Thanksgiving evening, then out of nowhere Dave wanting a divorce, the snake at the Java Hut, the sleepless night remembering Elvis Presley at the Ship Ahoy, and then in the morning Alice busy with Lauren's wedding, and Bryan coming, and the house so full of magi—"So that's why I'm here with you, Aunt Ethel, for no telling how long."

"What kind of snake was it?" asked Ethel.

"No, no, no. It's not about snakes, it's about feelings. We're supposed to be thinking about feelings. And maybe Dave is right. Thirty-three years ago it was Elvis Presley at the Ship Ahoy, and now it's just a turkey carcass left too long on simmer."

Ethel sat, her eyes little slits of concentration, thinking. Then she said, "Life is like work and consists of motions in sequence. You must use the momentum built up doing one operation to power the next."

There didn't seem to be any need to discuss it further after that, so they started to decorate the Christmas tree. Ethel set the timer.

"It used to take me nearly thirty-five minutes to decorate the tree," she said, "but then I came up with this." It was a block of wood with an eighteen-penny nail driven through it. Ethel laid the Christmas tree on its side, and with a couple of whacks she punched the tip of the nail into the butt end of the tree trunk. She stood the tree up at the edge of the porch, climbed the steps, and clipped the end of a string of lights to the top of the tree with a clothespin. "Watch this. This takes ten minutes off the total decorating time." She gave the tree a little shove, and it spun slowly on the nail, twirling the string of lights evenly from top to bottom. "Open the door." Ethel stood the tree up in the corner, plugged in the lights, and stood back. The tree leaned a little to the right. "Now that is just beautiful." She checked the time and noted it down. "I've got Christmas down to about forty-five minutes, total time."

"Life is like work and consists of motions in sequence," Ethel had said, but Sally did not feel that she was moving with purpose, but as if she were wandering around aimlessly, lost in an odd parenthetical stretch of time removed from before and after. At school everything was swept up into Christmas–silver glitter, Elmer's glue, "Up on the Housetop," "Silent Night," and all the eager children crazed by anticipation and advertisement. Getting divorced was the same as falling in love in a way, she discovered. Everywhere she went she felt that people could just look at her and tell. It must show.

And it did. Her principal called her in and said, "Sally, if you need time . . ." The lunchroom lady baked her a nine-by-thirteen-inch coconut cake. After the party when a little student threw up his red punch and green Rice Krispies squares, Dolores, her helper, said, "Mrs. Lewis, you go sit down and rest yourself and let me clean this up." Then it was all merry merry and happy happy, the first cold snap, and the last day of school.

"Now is when the rats move in," said Ethel, and she got out her old Blue Horse notebook of rat-trap histories and her collection of wire traps–funnel traps, trapdoor traps, and drop traps. In the long evenings as they sat in the glow of the Christmas tree, Ethel would oil the hinges in the traps and talk about rats, and Sally would stare into the fire and think about her married life. In her head she worked out little exercises in terrifying arithmetic: thirty-three years—she had probably been married to Dave longer than the years she had left to live.

"It is a wonderful rat, the pack rat," Ethel said, "strong, wily, vigorous, with a keen intelligence—and the most destructive rat known to man." She leafed through her notebook. "In February of 1965, in one three-hour period between two and five a.m., a single rat completely destroyed the wiring in your uncle M's new Dodge. And on December thirtieth, 1972, a rat chewed the bottom corner off a heart-pine door, got into a closet, and shredded a Navajo blanket, two down quilts, and a wedding dress."

What a fascinating creature an old marriage is! Sally thought. From its little, squirming beginning all those years ago at the Ship Ahoy it had changed over time into this highly evolved being. Buffeted by the demands of married life, useful traits had been selected for, modified, and strengthened. Dave's sultry sluggishness that had been so attractive in courtship had been honed by need into an admirable, stoic patience. And what had been in her youth a nearsighted preoccupation with detail had turned into a useful efficiency that they both counted on. Other traits, of diminishing usefulness, such as that Elvis Presley falling in love, were almost gone, hardly noticeable now—but still there in a way, like the little vestigial leg bones embedded in the body wall of a whale.

And here their marriage was today, after all those adaptive shifts—a funny-looking, old thing, surely, with splayed toes and eyes on the top of its head, but elegantly suited to its ecological niche.

"What could Dave be thinking?" Sally said to herself. A divorce in such a marriage would be like the extinction of a species.

Late that night Sally heard a thump, an anticipatory pause, then another thump and a pause, then three in a row—*thumpthumpthump.* From the far side of the house she could barely hear the response: thump, thump, *thumpthumpthump.* The rats had moved in.

The next day Ethel baited and set out the traps. "These rats are nobody's fool," she said, and sure enough, that afternoon it turned gray and dismal, a mean rain fell until dark, and the temperature dropped forty degrees.

"This is just like the first freeze of 1950," said Ethel. "This will be a good year for trapping rats."

Just before midnight Sally heard the rustling sound, a tentative testing—a soft nudge on metal, then the flap of the trapdoor, and the panicked scrambling. The lights came on, and there was Ethel, wild-eyed and triumphant in her chaotic floral bathrobe with her white hair shoved up both sides of her head.

"Look at that!" she said, tilting the trap so the rat ran up the side. "A big bull rat. Look at that coat, look at the gleam in his eye—the size of him!" She looked at the rat and the rat looked at her. "I don't think I've ever caught a finer-looking rat.

"We have to turn him loose way out from civilization. A rat like this can travel ten miles in a day and destroy an entire household in one night. You drive."

She put the rat trap on the backseat and covered it with an old sheet, "for his privacy," she said, and they drove off through the empty, silent streets. They drove through the downtown, with the swags of colored lights across the street. They drove past the park, with all the trees outlined in white lights. No other cars were out in this cold at this hour, and it seemed as if all this show had been put on just for them—Ethel, Sally, and the rat.

"There's my street," said Sally, and without thinking she turned and drove past the Harlands' tired, old reindeer, past the Shaws', who always just put up the one string of lights on the eaves of the porch, and past the Stewarts', who had gone wild a few years back when the icicle lights first came out.

"Look," said Sally, "the lamp is on in the living room, Dave must still be up. No Christmas decorations, poor Dave, his heart wouldn't be in it. Look at him, there he is sitting in his easy chair with his cowboy hat on."

"Why in the world is he wearing that big black cowboy hat?" said Ethel. "In the house, and this late at night."

"Well, I guess just like me, Dave can't sleep."

"Looka there, who is that little girl?"

From the direction of the bedroom a young woman came into view. She leaned over the back of Dave's chair, and a cascade of bright hair hid their kiss.

Sally sat there with the engine idling, staring. It was like watching something shameful on television where no matter how much you know you should, you just can't make yourself turn it off.

"That's not a little girl," said Sally. "That's the red-haired woman who mixes paint at the True Value Hardware." She watched Dave's hand slide down the side of the chair and fumble for the handle, and then with one smooth stroke, as if he were easing the gear-shift lever of a fine automobile into overdrive, he slid the chair into full recline. The black cowboy hat fell on the floor.

"Chuck Brinson told Dave one time he looked just like Ted Turner in that cowboy hat," said Sally.

Then, just like Christmas lights, thoughts came on in Sally's head, twinkling, twinkling. Just as one went off, another came on. "Why, she's no older than Lauren!" one thought twinkled. Then "She's the same age I was all those years ago at the Ship Ahoy!" lit up and was gone. There was a twinkle, and Dave was on the roof of the lunchroom with the gleam of the sheet metal lighting up his golden hair. Another twinkle and there was Dave in a field of broom sedge hollering, "Whoa!" to a long-legged dog named Leroy. One more twinkle and they were in the emergency room with Addie. Then there was nothing left but Dave in his easy chair, and the redheaded girl from True Value draping herself over him. All the twinkling lights were gone, and instead there was just a comforting darkness, and a wonderful weightless feeling, as if all this time up until right now that snake had been on *her* shoulders.

"Give me that rat," Sally said, and she stepped out of the car, opened the back door, and slid the trap out. Straight, tall, and strong, she strode up the front walkway, knelt down at the camellia hedge, and lifted the trapdoor. The rat, confused and disoriented, scrabbled against the back of the trap for just a second. Then he righted himself, made a brief assessing pause, and darted out of the trap. Across the strip of lawn he ran, sleek and fast, and disappeared under the White Emperor camellia at the corner of the front steps.

The Telephone Man

ESSIE AND HELEN were two old sisters who lived together in their childhood home, and Arthur was a man with only one hand who had been in love with Essie for as long as anyone could remember.

"You know that one hand can do almost anything," he said to Helen. They were in the house, rolling out the living room rug, and Essie was out in the yard trying to mow a clearing in the tall weeds beyond the bird feeder with a little push mower. She wanted a vista, just like the one she had seen at Birdsong Nature Center. But the grass was too thick, and the lawn mower kept choking down.

"The one hand has nothing to do with it, Arthur," said Helen. "You know that. It's just Essie. She's not a marrying woman."

"And what the hand can't do, the knob can do," said Arthur. Instead of the hook so famous in jokes and horror stories, Arthur had a wooden knob he had carved himself out of a live-oak knot. "I can drive nails with it."

"It's not the knob or the hand or anything at all to do with you, Arthur." Helen was the sweet one. Essie did everything the same way she mowed that grass, straight ahead and all screwed up with concentration.

The mower choked down again and they watched Essie viciously pull the starter cord. The mower coughed and sputtered, and soon as it settled down to run, Essie shoved it into the tall grass, *uuhhnn uuhhnn.* She was wearing a loose denim dress and black hiking boots.

"Uh," said Arthur, "it hurts me to hear a small engine labor like that. She needs more horsepower than what she's got. She needs a Yazoo or a Snapping Turtle. What she really needs is that old Gravely mower your dad used to have. Where is that old Gravely mower?"

That was the first day of fall, and that evening was the first cool night. Essie was bedded down in the sofa under a down quilt reading about abutilon in the Plant Delights nursery catalog, and Helen was painting a picture of lemons, waiting for the damp spot on the paper to be just right so she could get the stippled skin of the lemon in one stroke.

"It's painful to see how hard he works trying to please you," she said to Essie. "You admire a big goldfish in the courthouse fountain, and Arthur digs a pond with that one hand and a shovel; you read a letter from Dorothy Wordsworth, and Arthur goes out and plants a hundred daffodils; now you want a mowed vista, and Arthur's been out in the barn all afternoon trying to resurrect that giant mowing machine that's been sitting up on blocks since Daddy died."

"Arthur plants everything too deep," said Essie.

"You're too much alike, you and Arthur. You neither one of you give up on anything, even when you should."

Then the telephone rang. "I can't leave this lemon," said Helen, and Essie was tangled up in the quilt. There were the three rings, then the digital-sounding voice they had for the outgoing message, then the tone, and a man's voice, deep and weary, said, "Hey, baby. I know it's been a long time . . ." A sigh and a pause.

"'Baby'!" said Essie, and she sat up and leaned toward the telephone. Her catalog slid to the floor.

"I know I done wrong," the voice said. "I just want to let you know I'm going to get out of this mess before long, and I'm sorry for what I done. Call me."

"Poor thing," said Helen. "He's got the wrong number and he doesn't know it." She took up her brush and stroked the yellow onto the shaded side of the lemon. Essie picked up her catalog and lay back in the sofa, but the pages had flipped from *a* to *x*, and she lay there for a long time staring at the xanthosomas. "'Baby'!" she whispered.

"Just probably some girlfriend trouble," said Helen. "He'll get it figured out."

The next morning at first light Arthur was back in the barn taking the mower apart. It was an old Gravely mower from the 1940s, and it had not run since Mr. Baker died in 1970. Rats had chewed up the wiring, the belts and tires were rotten and crumbling, and when Arthur opened the hood, lizards came skittering out. All morning Essie and Helen heard rattling and clanging, and at noon Arthur came in covered with grease, wiping his hand on a rag he had safety-pinned to his belt loop. He had scrubbed all the gummed-up oil out of the air cleaner with a toothbrush and laid it out on a rag in the sun to dry, and he had taken the carburetor apart and had the float bowl, the needle valve, and the sediment bowl soaking in a coffee can of kerosene. Essie and Helen came out and stood with their hands clutched against their bellies and peered down at the mower.

"Looka here," said Arthur. "This is the whole fuel system, all varnished up from old gas. I've got to get all this cleaned up and cut a new gasket for the sediment bowl and the carburetor. I've got to get all this rust and trash out of the gas tank and see can't I get some fire out of this magneto, then this old Gravely will mow anything you want mowed. This is a fine, fine machine! This old Gravely will mow down all those little sweet gums coming up in there, all that sumac, that Bahia grass that would choke down any other mower, this Gravely will mow it. I'll mow the whole thing, right up to the fence wire!"

"No," said Essie, drawing shapes in the air with her arms. "I just want a swath from the bird feeder, curving around the camellia bushes and out into the sunny place, just like at Birdsong."

"Arthur, quit working on this old thing," said Helen. "It's too much for just that little bit of mowing. Essie can get Randy to come over with his Bush Hog on Saturday and mow that strip for twenty-five dollars."

"He'd scalp it," said Arthur. "You watch. I'll have this thing purring like a kitten by Saturday. This is a fine old machine. They don't make them like this anymore."

That night when the breeze would blow just right, they could smell a whiff of gasoline through the open windows. Essie was in the living room and Helen was in the kitchen making a tomato sandwich when the telephone rang, but Essie didn't answer it. She stopped and stood in the middle of the room through the three rings, the outgoing message, then that voice, tired and sorrowful. "I'm in a bad place, baby, I need to talk to you."

"Essie, pick it up and tell that man we are not his girlfriend, he needs to check the number," said Helen.

"I want to hear this," said Essie.

"I'll make it up to you, baby, I swear I will," said the telephone man. "Call me."

The next morning Arthur was back, and he worked all that day and the next day with his mind the whole time on just two things: one, the Gravely mower; and two, Essie. Every now and then a little shred of a thought would work its way to the surface and he would be moved to sing out a word or a phrase, and all afternoon Helen and her little painting students on the porch would hear, "Elberta peach!" or "Ag tires from Axelrod's!" or "'Rave On'!"

Nothing with Strings

For most of one afternoon he thought about a day fifty years ago out at Reed Pond, the day he fell in love with Essie and never got over it. Essie in her black bathing suit, eating an Elberta peach. Arthur could bring that day up in his mind anytime he wanted to and see it just as clear: the pickerelweed and cypress trees on the far bank, the sparkle on the water, then the posts of the dock and the wet and dry spots, then Essie and her laughing eyes, the way she looked at him right before her teeth sank into that Elberta peach. Then moving on from there, his own hands on his knees—both of them in those days—and on Johnny Lovett's transistor radio that he was so proud of, Buddy Holly singing "Rave On."

That day was the beginning of it, and everything had started changing on that day and never stopped changing from then on: Essie gone off to college and becoming a demonstrator, Helen in New York City an artist, and Reed Pond now called Mirror Lake, with lawn grass where the cypress trees used to be and houses all around it, each one as big as the Taj Mahal.

Just one thing hadn't changed, and never would change. Even when he was fighting the war and she was marching up and down the streets of Madison, Wisconsin, waving a peace sign, he wrote Essie a letter every week and signed every one of them "Love, Arthur." And when she took up with that dope-smoking Yankee artist who drew pictures of little bright-colored people with big feet on every flat surface and Arthur got sent home with one hand, every time she came back he would go over there and sit in her daddy's kitchen and say, "Essie, I love you." Then there was that wispy boy from New Mexico who called himself a musician, though all he did was a lot of strumming in two chords, long, long songs that didn't have any subject matter. Arthur knew how he treated Essie, and when she finally left him and came back home to get her bearings, Arthur came over and stood on the bottom step while she looked at him from behind the screen door with her face swollen and sad. Arthur said, "If he hurts you, Essie, I'll kill him, one hand or no hands. You know I'll take care of you till the day you die, because I love you."

But all Essie ever said was "Arthur, Arthur," and she was gone again and stayed gone this time.

Helen was the one who would talk to him about it, saying over and over, "She's not the marrying kind, Arthur," and "She likes change and excitement, Arthur," and probably the truest thing Helen ever said: "You're an old friend, Arthur, and Essie likes things to be new."

The first time Arthur ever heard of a bagel, Helen told him Essie was working in a bagel shop in Spokane, Washington, and when he saw one in a grocery store, he bought it and stood in the parking lot and gnawed and gnawed until he had eaten the whole thing, just so he would know what Essie was doing. Then Helen said she had quit the bagels and was putting harpsichords together in Vermont, then was in the bottom of the Grand Canyon living with Indians. After a long gap of years, finally a letter came from Helen a year ago saying, "Dear Arthur, we are two tired old lady sisters, and we're moving back home." And there they were again, just as they'd started, Essie and Helen back in that house, Helen still painting her pictures, and Essie with her gray hair all piled up and deaf in one ear, but Essie still Essie.

Now! thought Arthur, and all year he dug fish ponds and planted daffodils and cleared out brush.

"Now!" he said, wiping his knob against his pant leg. "Now! First thing tomorrow morning, get those ag tires from Axelrod's, hook up the spark plug—she's got gas, she's got fire, she's got air, she's got to run!"

He put up his tools, spread a tarpaulin over the whole thing, and came up on the porch. The telephone was ringing.

"Arthur, come up here and let me fix you a cup of coffee," said Helen. She called, "Essie, get the phone! Arthur, come over to the sink, I'll wash your hand with some of this orange cleaner."

The telephone rang again, but Essie didn't answer it.

She sat down in a chair in the middle of the room with both her feet on the floor and her elbows on her knees, leaning toward the telephone.

"I'm in a real dark place," the voice said. "Baby, please call me." Then there was the click and the dial tone.

For a while they just stood there not saying anything, Helen holding the tub of orange cleaner at the sink, and Arthur wiping his knob with the greasy rag over and over. Then Arthur said, "No thank you, Helen, I'll just go on home."

✦

The next day was the perfect fall day, bright and cool, with a high blue sky and the welcome smell of a change of season—the tea-olive trees in their first full bloom, scuppernong grapes and pine straw heated up by the sun, and soon with all that, the smell of mown grass.

From the house Essie and Helen could hear the Gravely mower, running just as smooth, and from the porch they could see through the crape-myrtle shade out into the sunny place Arthur perched up on the sulky behind the Gravely mower, looping around and around, mowing just the shape Essie had drawn in the air, first his back on the loop going out, then his face on the loop coming back, every now and then turning to look over his shoulder at the mowed stripe unfurling behind the mower like a green grosgrain ribbon.

On the porch Helen finished her lemon picture and propped it up on the railing to look at it. The hardest part had turned out to be the best: a place where the knife had peeled too deep and it seemed you could look down through the clear layers of yellow and into the deep heart of the lemon.

Essie finished filling out her order form: three abutilons from Plant Delights nursery, and still they heard the mower, near and far and near again, then farther and farther away.

"Seems like he's been mowing a mighty long time for that little bit of field," said Helen. "We need to go out there and admire it for Arthur."

"We need to go out there and be sure he hasn't mowed everything down," said Essie. "You know how he is."

They walked out just the way the eye was drawn into that garden, through the dappled shade of the crape myrtle, around the dense green of the camellias, and into the sunny place. "Oh, good," said Helen, "Arthur's taking a rest in the shade."

"But the mower's still running," said Essie.

"He's probably scared to shut it off for fear it won't start up again. . . . Arthur, it's beautiful!" Helen called. "Absolutely beautiful!"

But Arthur wasn't taking a rest. Arthur was lying stone dead, half in the shade and half in the sun, right where he had fallen off that Gravely mower when the heart attack hit him. The part of him that was in the sun was warm, and the part of him that was in the shade was cool.

After all the gasping was over, and the cries of "Arthur, oh, Arthur!" and the hopeless attempts at resuscitation, and a little weeping, Essie and Helen tried to turn Arthur over to get him into a more lifelike position, but his knees buttressed him, and he wouldn't roll. They gave up and just stood there, looking down at him lying on the mowed grass, just as they had looked down into the engine of the Gravely mower, with their hands clasped to their bellies. His eyes were open, and he had a look on his face of wonder and delight, as if he had just bitten into something unexpectedly good.

"I'll stay here with him," said Helen. "I'll cover him up with something. You go call that cousin in Woodberry, and 911 or whoever you're supposed to call."

Just as Essie came around the crape-myrtle tree the telephone started ringing, and by the time she got to the porch steps there was that familiar voice talking on the answering machine.

Essie was not the kind to cry, but now the tears began to flow. She picked up the telephone and without any greeting or pause she cried out in a rough, choked voice, "Arthur is dead! And no one at this number wants to hear from you, ever again!" Then she slammed the receiver down and banged out the screen door and sat down on the steps.

Out through the vista she could just see Helen sitting on the mowed grass, and there they sat for a long time, two old ladies clutching their knees, with a dead man between them, and in the background the sound of the Gravely mower, first a steady hum, then a sputter and a cough as it ran out of gas, then just birdsong—a cardinal calling from the feeder, the loud tweet of a wren in the tea-olive tree, then in the distance the thin, wavering whistle of the white-throated sparrow, the first one of the season.

Miss Wigglesworth's Bull

THIS IS A STORY about a middle-aged woman named Miss Wigglesworth and the Jersey bull she won in a raffle. The story takes place about ninety years ago, when roads were not paved, and country children could not get to the schools in town. Miss Wigglesworth lived with one of these country families and worked as a teacher for their children.

Miss Wigglesworth was a homely woman. Her skin and her eyes and her hair were all the same color, a dim, pasty tan, with a vague nose in the middle of it all, and such big front teeth that her upper lip had to work to keep them covered. She dressed in pale, flimsy clothes and she was always plucking at fringed shawls and scarves and gathered sleeves, trying to get them to drape in graceful folds. But the folds always seemed to come untucked or unpinned, and frazzled tails of fabric would trail after her, snagging on things.

Miss Wigglesworth took her job of civilizing these country children seriously. She would not allow the boys to sing about the Waxful Maid, whose sweetheart took her by her golden hair and drug her on the ground, then threw her into the river that flows through Waxful town. Instead she sat them down in straight-backed chairs and made them memorize long poems about well-dressed little boys who would hear the songs of angels in the night and sweetly die before dawn.

She thought she could tame the girls by having them play with dolls. But they were rough little girls who had never owned a doll, so the resourceful Miss Wigglesworth would go out at dusk and catch a few fat toad-frogs and sit up all night sewing little outfits for them with silk thread. In the schoolroom the next morning she and the girls would dress the toad-frogs up, tugging their little, nubbly, crooked arms through the ruffled sleeves and tying tiny silken bows under their gray, dank throats. By the time the toad-frogs were fully dressed in all their finery, they would be half-dead from the handling and would sit quite docilely in their little twig chairs. Miss Wigglesworth would arrange this grisly tableau in the middle of the schoolroom table—the mother, the father, and the boy and the girl toad-frogs, their grave dark eyes looking solemnly out from under their bonnets and hats, their struggles calmed by now to pitiful gestures of graceful desperation.

"There now," Miss Wigglesworth would say, snipping a final thread and clapping her hands with delight. "Such a happy little family!"

On some summer afternoons, when the children longed to be killing rats against time down at the barn or baiting hogs back in the river swamp, Miss Wigglesworth would make them accompany her on a slow stroll through the garden, where they would suddenly come up on a complete tea service hidden behind a clump of aspidistra—cups and saucers, lace napkins, little silver spoons, and iced cakes with ants crawling on them.

"Oh, look!" Miss Wigglesworth would exclaim, striking a carefully rehearsed pose denoting surprise and delight, her eyes stretched wide, one hand pressed to her bosom. "The dear little fairies have set out this tea party just for us!"

But the children knew this was a lie. They had seen Miss Wigglesworth with their own eyes earnestly staggering out to the end of the garden over and over with the tea tray, the fringes of her shawl snagging on branches, her upper lip straining gently to cover her teeth in her excitement. They did not want to sit on these uncomfortable garden seats on a sweltering summer afternoon swallowing scalding-hot tea out of rose-painted cups and listening to Miss Wigglesworth remind them, "Pinkie, pinkie!"

That night the fairy tea party would be matched with a little act of cruelly imaginative revenge, and the next morning Miss Wigglesworth would be sitting in the hall on her strapped-up trunk, dressed in her traveling cloak, her hat on her head. "I cannot allow myself to be . . . ," she would say in a quavering voice, and then the mother of the children would sweetly say, "Oh, Miss Wigglesworth" and "Dear Miss Wigglesworth." And the father, stern and tall and somber, would say, "Miss Wigglesworth, will you step into my office please." And there in that dark and serious room a little, red-eyed child would stand in front of the gun cabinet facing Miss Wigglesworth and, with her fists clenched behind her back, recite, "Miss Wigglesworth, I am sorry I put that very small alligator in your bathtub, and I will not do it again, ma'am."

Later that day the mother would find a time to be alone with Miss Wigglesworth and, tweaking a drooping shawl back into position on Miss Wigglesworth's bony shoulder, would say, "Miss Wigglesworth, you know we love you and appreciate you very much, but sometimes I wonder . . . for someone in your position . . . if you fully realize how fortunate . . . living as you do in the bosom of our family, why I know girls who would . . . Now we are very happy to have you here of course, and . . . Oh, Miss Wigglesworth, dear Miss Wigglesworth, don't start that."

And the next day things would go on just as before, because the fact was, Miss Wigglesworth, for all her strapped-up trunk and her traveling cloak and her statements about not allowing herself to be . . . , had nowhere to go.

One morning at the breakfast table, laying her knife and fork down for emphasis and waiting for everyone's complete attention, the mother announced, "Children"—and she gave them a squelching glare—"we were very pleased to learn last night that Miss Wigglesworth has won a bull."

It was not something that one expected to hear about Miss Wigglesworth, and there was a moment of silence while Miss Wigglesworth dabbed at her teeth daintily with a napkin and blushed with pride. "Miss Hamilton herself presented me with the gift," she said.

Miss Hamilton was an eccentric Yankee spinster of the prominent Pennsylvania Hamiltons, who, in the poor days after the War Between the States, had swept down South from Philadelphia and bought the old Baggett place. She had made the house elegant with chandeliers and Persian rugs, and then, blessed with money to indulge her whims, she had turned the tired, old cotton plantation into an elegant little dairy, with whitewashed fences enclosing flowery meadows, green-and-white milking parlors with Ionic columns, and cows imported from the Isle of Jersey. As a kind of goodwill gesture to her poor neighbors, when the cement was dry on the serpentine brick walls and the stone drinking troughs were filled with water and the highbred Jersey cows were settled down from their Atlantic crossing, Miss Hamilton held a kind of jamboree. Long tables with linen tablecloths were set up in the meadows, lined with silver pitchers of iced creamy drinks, and Blue Willow platters piled high with buttered sandwiches and cakes and cookies in the shape of cows. At the height of the festivities Miss Hamilton herself appeared on an upstairs balcony, dressed in a kind of Marie Antoinette milkmaid costume, with a silk satin dirndl skirt and ruffled pantaloons, and selected the winning raffle ticket from a gleaming brass milk pail.

"And our Miss Wigglesworth," said the mother, smiling down the table, "was the happy winner of a week-old Jersey bull calf!"

No one told Miss Wigglesworth that a bull calf in a dairy herd is useless, something to be gotten rid of, like chicken litter from an egg farm. And he was an adorable little thing, as all week-old calves must be, a delicate fawn color, with smudges of black around his shiny eyes and a black, shiny nose always poking for something to suck.

Miss Wigglesworth was devoted to him. She fed him four times a day from a bucket with a rubber nipple at the bottom of it; she wove daisy chains to hang around his neck and marigold crowns for his head. There was no time for fairy tea parties, and it got to be December without "Ode to Autumn" being memorized as Miss Wigglesworth trudged back and forth from the springhouse to the barn with her milk bucket. The time to castrate the little bull came and went, but no one thought of it, and before long, in spite of his size, he began to behave like a bull, rearing back and lowering his head between his scrawny shoulders, swatting his tail from side to side, and pawing up dirt with a tiny hoof.

Of course Miss Wigglesworth named him Toro, and when she wasn't looking, the children would climb into the paddock and flick a red rag in his face and shout, "Toro! Toro!" Then, when the little bull got so big that they could no longer snatch him up by the front legs and prance him around, or grab him by his little nubs of horns and fling him over on his side, they left off the red rag and took to tormenting the young bull from the loft overhead, where they would lie in the hay, calling, "Toro! Toro!" The bull would snort and stomp and ramp from one end of the fence to the other, looking for them, and they would throw sticks down on him.

After a year he had grown to his full height, and by the time he was two years old he had filled out, with a hump on his massive shoulders. The delicate shadings on his face darkened and spread so that the powerful front parts of him were a gleaming black. He grew out of his capers and twirls and feints, and now he mostly just stood in the middle of his little paddock, glowering out through the fence and munching the armfuls of tender grass Miss Wigglesworth brought him from the edge of the pond. The children stopped throwing sticks at him, and instead, grown men would come and lean on the fence and gaze in at him and say, "Uunh-unh." Miss Wigglesworth's bull would leave off his chewing, make a slow turn, lower his head, and glare at the men out of all that darkness. The dust would settle and everything would grow still. It seemed as if even the birds would stop singing, until there was nothing left but the sunshine and the bull's stare, and finally the men would turn away from the fence and say, "Whoa!"

At the end of three years the bull was moved to a woods pasture at the back of the place. Miss Wigglesworth trudged back there faithfully every evening to leave a bucket of corn and oats at the gate, but the bull stayed for the most part at the far end of the pasture, a dark shape among trees. Occasionally people would see him in the distance and point him out. "Oh, look," they would say, as if they had almost forgotten, "Miss Wigglesworth's bull!"

This is a story about a bull, so it has to happen: the summer afternoon; the child, hot and tired, taking a shortcut through the woods. Nothing to it really, just a twitch of that hump, a flick of that head, and then a little heap of child in the grass. Then the long night of dread and fear, with the doctor padding in and out of the dark room pronouncing that terrible word *coma*.

In the morning though, just before dawn, the child opened his eyes, stirred under the sheets, and asked for a drink of water. Dread turned into joy, and fear turned into rage, and at first light the father took his gun and marched himself across the fields to the woods pasture. There was nothing to it really, just the crack of a rifle shot and a thud, and then a great heap of bull in the dewy grass. Miss Wigglesworth, a dim, fluttering presence at the edge of it all, was not even consulted.

By afternoon the child was up, looking precious and frail and being made much of. The story was told over and over to friends and relatives, who would pinch his cheeks and ruffle his hair and gasp and smack and say, "Bless his heart" and "What a miracle," while in the backyard chunks of Miss Wigglesworth's bull bobbed and simmered in a vat over a fire and slowly melted off the bones. In the evening buckets of cornmeal were stirred into the slurry with long ash paddles, and a handful of salt was thrown in, and the whole mess was dipped out and packed into lard cans as dog food.

The very next day three men drove up in the yard—the manager of Miss Hamilton's dairy herd, a Mr. Sharples from Philadelphia, and a representative from the American Jersey Cattle Club. They stood around in their dark, foreign-looking clothes until the father showed them into his office.

For a long time there was just a lot of talk about the dairy business and Jersey cows, importation records, and the Herd Improvement Registry. Then the talk turned specifically to Miss Hamilton's little dairy herd. Testing procedures for measuring and recording butterfat production had been pioneered there, and it had been discovered that cows in Miss Wigglesworth's bull's breeding line were amazingly productive—so productive in fact that for breeding purposes Miss Wigglesworth's bull was, well, in short, they were interested, very interested, if the father would consider—and since he was not a dairyman himself—

"But you see—," said the father.

"We are very interested in acquiring this animal, sir," said Mr. Sharples from Philadelphia.

"Maybe you don't realize the importance of . . . ," said the representative of the American Jersey Cattle Club, and there was a lengthy explanation of the Babcock Butterfat Test.

"But—," the father said.

"Sir," said the manager of Miss Hamilton's dairy, "Miss Hamilton is prepared to pay a considerable sum."

"But you must not know what has happened here," said the father. "That bull—"

"A small fortune in fact, sir," said Mr. Sharples from Philadelphia.

◆

"Damn Yankees," said the mother at the supper table that night, gripping her knife and fork in tight fists, "coming into our house with their talk of small fortunes." She beamed across the table at her son, seated like a little prince on a chair with a tasseled cushion, who still managed a limp when he remembered.

"But," Miss Wigglesworth started up in a quavering voice, "the bull . . . the small fortune . . ."

"Miss Wigglesworth!" the mother said in a withering tone. "This has nothing to do with you!" And she swept down on her son with kisses, saying, "No Yankee's small fortune can pay for my child's life!"

It was much later that someone, maybe a maid or a gardener, missed Miss Wigglesworth.

"She's moping over that . . . animal," snapped the mother, and someone was sent to the woods pasture to find her. They looked in the garden, they looked in the barn.

Finally someone thought to check Miss Wigglesworth's room. Her clothes, her Bible and *Book of Inspirational Verses,* her plaster statue of the Three Graces, her filigree-glass basket, and her trunk, all were gone. There was not even a sliver of soap on the wash-hand stand.

"Without so much as a by-your-leave!" snapped the mother, remembering the other melodramatic scenes of departure: the buttoned-up cloak, the strapped-up trunk, and then the sniveling and the tears. "You watch—she'll be back."

But Miss Wigglesworth did not come back. In fact, Miss Wigglesworth was never seen or heard from again.

◆

The accident with the bull was just the first of a series of misfortunes the family suffered during the next year. Pine beetles spread from one lightning-struck tree throughout a vast tract of old longleaf pines, and they all had to be cut and sold as salvage. Then there was a wet winter, and rain rushing down the bare slope where the woods had been eroded gullies through the fields, and all the topsoil ended up spread out in a muddy flat down at the river. And then, early one morning, the house burned to the ground. No one was hurt, and they managed to save a few pieces of furniture, but it was a fine old house, built in the 1830s out of heart pine, and it made a spectacular fire.

The father's pride went with the house, and he sold his ruined land to a paper company and got a job at Miss Hamilton's thriving dairy as a pastureman, where he became quite respected among agronomists for improving grazing by intercropping grasses with velvet bean.

But the mother was never comfortable in her new, small life in the rented cottage at the dairy. Her greatest pleasure was in telling and retelling her bored neighbors about the grand life she had led when she had been mistress of a plantation and had had servants and a governess for the children.

"A Miss Wigglesworth, tiresome woman, always giving herself airs."

The neighbor's eyes would flicker and he would lean forward with his hands on his knees and say, "Well . . ."

But by then the mother would have come to the accident with the bull. "My son not expected to live through the night, but by a miracle . . . ," and the neighbor would settle back down, knowing there would be no escape now until after the house burned to the ground.

". . . burned to the ground, one of the finest houses in the county, all heart pine."

And the neighbor would stretch and begin to rise. "Well, it's been real nice, and give your husband my regards."

"Such a coincidence, the fire exactly a year and a day after the accident."

And knowing the rest by heart, the neighbor would prompt, "It must have been something in the–"

"There we stood, at first light, our feet wet with dew, watching our ancestral home go up in flames. The cause of the fire was never determined," the mother would conclude all in her own time. "It must have been something in the wiring."

Bus Ride

"THERE WILL BE no smoking on the bus," the driver announced, settling himself with practiced care into his seat. "If you've got a radio, use the headphones and keep the volume down. If you must chew gum, don't pop it. And there will be no profanity, because there are ladies on the bus. We will be making stops in Dooley, Midway, Choctawhatchee, Snipes, High Ridge, Cottonville, Chancey, Bonnie View, Despera Springs, and Pensacola. Watch your step walking to and from the restroom." Then he flapped his sun visor down and we made that snub-nosed turn into Tennessee Street and headed west into a late-fall afternoon.

There weren't many people on the bus—just me in the front; across the aisle in the handicapped seat a dismal old man in cheap, worn-out clothes, whose mind was gone; and farther back a little boy traveling alone, with his hair parted neatly and combed wet, looking anxious and alert.

It was one of those late-fall afternoons when you can feel the lingering sweet languor of summer in the air, but in the slant of light you can also see the first glimpse of winter with its exciting cold and mysterious dark. I felt honored to be heading west in the front seat of a bus on that day, scooping in that rare afternoon through the wide windshield.

In downtown Dooley, the first stop, only two new people got on: a young man with a battered guitar case, his shirt unbuttoned and a long, curved tooth hanging down his chest on a black cord; and a little old lady wearing a flowered print dress, a tan moth-eaten coat and matching hat, and short white gloves. The young man struck a pose in the middle of the aisle with his legs spread, flung his greasy blond hair over his shoulder, and said, "Y'all ready for some music? 'Cause I'm here now."

"Watch it, son," warned the bus driver, and the young man swaggered down the aisle thumping the plaid backs of the seats and twitching his shoulders, then sat down across from the earnest little boy. The lady settled down in the front seat, arranged the folds of her coat carefully, turned to me, and said, "I have been to Dooley for a sad occasion. I have been to Dooley for the funeral of my brother-in-law's wife."

We turned around and around and around the Gadsden County courthouse and headed west again on 90.

"You sing songs?" the little boy asked the man with the guitar.

"Sing songs?" said the man. "What do you mean, 'sing songs'?" Then he threw himself into a little rhythmic convulsion of thumping, tapping, and twitching. "I am a man of music. In fact, I am made out of music, body and soul. You cut me open, you know what you'll find?"

"Guts?" said the little boy.

"Music! I am a man of music. I am just like Carl Perkins. Carl Perkins went to a dance, heard a boy tell a girl, 'Don't step on my blue suede shoes,' came right home and took three potatoes out of a sack, and wrote the world's most famous song right on the side of that grocery bag. Did you know that?"

"My mama took her pocketbook to the grocery store and she never came back," said the little boy.

"Me and Carl Perkins," said the man. "I see something, I hear a song. I can't help it. I'm a man of music."

We rode along for a little while then without talking, past weedy fields scrubby from drought, pecan groves, house trailers, and every now and then an old homestead with a crumbling chimney sticking up out of a thicket of leggy azaleas, and a Confederate rose in the side yard, full of frilly pink blossoms. Midway came and went—a little, closed-up town and some trash in the road, but it wasn't much of a day for traveling and nobody else got on the bus. The little lady began to read a book of advice on how to live a noble life, one suggestion for each day of the year. The old man across from us slumped in his seat with his cheap acrylic sweater rucked up under his arms, gazing out the window, but no matter what went by, he didn't look at anything. The Man of Music twitched in his seat and drummed an elaborate beat with his feet on the floor, heel and toe. Every now and then he would come out with a volley of thumps on the seatback and a snatch of a phrase: ". . . but uh-uh, honey, lay offa them shoes."

After Choctawhatchee the countryside flattened out into miles and miles of farmland and planted pines. We had changed to a new time zone on the long bridge over the Apalachicola River; it was an hour earlier, and the soporific scenery and the low sun shining in through the windshield made it seem as if that late-fall afternoon were riding along with us on the bus and would just last forever.

The bus driver began telling us how, as a twelve-year-old boy, he had fallen under the influence of Governor George Wallace at a rally in Opp, Alabama. "I was mesmerized by Governor Wallace. I just had to see him again, so the next day I got on the bus and rode up to Montgomery to the governor's mansion."

"Knock me down, step on my face," sang the Man of Music.

The little lady marked her place in her book with a velvet ribbon, closed it in her lap, turned to me, and said, "You may be wondering why I'm wearing these short white gloves."

The little boy said, "My daddy said he should have known something wasn't right when she took that big old pocketbook to the grocery store when all she needed was a can of tuna fish and a box of crackers."

"I didn't know any better," said the bus driver. "I didn't know a twelve-year-old boy couldn't just walk right into the governor's mansion and say, 'I come to see the governor.' So I just did it."

"When you're a man of music you don't even need an instrument," said the Man of Music. "You can make music out of anything. Did you know that Carl Perkins's first guitar was made out of nothing but a cigar box and a broomstick?"

"My granny keeps her money in a cigar box," said the little boy. "She don't have a big pocketbook."

"So I just did it," said the bus driver. "I'd sneak off from home two, three times a week and ride the bus up to Montgomery. 'I come to see the governor,' I'd say. Pretty soon they started getting used to me, they let me come on in. I'd just sit there in his office and visit with him, just me and Governor Wallace."

In the seat next to us the old man had slumped down so far his knuckles were scraping the floor. "You need to sit up straight," the little lady told him. "You're gon' fall out in the floor. Do you want a cookie?" But the old man didn't seem able to do anything for himself, so at the next stop, High Ridge, the Man of Music came up to the front of the bus, stood in the aisle facing the old man, and hitched up his own britches. "I'm gon' straighten you up, old buddy," he said, and wrapped his arms around the old man and hauled him back upright.

"Pull his sweater down," said the little lady. "He's cold." The Man of Music pulled the sweater down over the old man's slack, bare belly and gave him a pat.

"Here," said the lady. "Give him a cookie."

The Man of Music said, not unkindly, "He don't want a cookie, ma'am," then squatted down and leaned over to get his face in the old man's sagging line of vision. "Old buddy, listen to me. Pretty soon me and you gon' get off this bus and smoke us a cigarette. Lucky Strike."

We paused at abandoned brick bus stations in Cottonville and Chancey, little tired-looking towns with only a few stores left open on the main street selling used vacuum cleaners and parts of agricultural equipment. In Bonnie View there was no bus station at all, just a little barbecue shack with a rusty metal awning casting some hot shade. In the back of the bus the Man of Music began talking about how women were mysteriously attracted to him.

"It's an invisible force," he said. "They flock to me everywhere I go, they can't help themselves."

"My daddy said she left because she couldn't be satisfied," said the little boy. "She had the can't-help-its, my daddy said."

"'Don't say can't! Can't never did a thing–,'" sang the Man of Music. "You know what they call me? They call me the Love Train. I'm a locomotive of love."

"You may be wondering why I'm wearing these short white gloves," said the little lady.

"It's something about women and a stringed instrument," said the Man of Music. "It's almost too easy—like shooting ducks over bait."

"My daddy can't play a stringed instrument," said the little boy. "He just works over at the silica mine."

"You see," said the little lady, "my brother-in-law's wife was a great one for making jams and jellies."

"Despera Springs!" said the bus driver. "Fifteen minutes, stretch your legs." He stopped the bus, cranked the door open, and stood up in the aisle and looked at each of us as if he were checking to see if we were all still there. "Ma'am," he said to the little lady, "fifteen-minute stop. You might want to stretch your legs. Fifteen-minute stop, young fellow," he said to the little boy. "Despera Springs. World's roundest lake, you might want to take a look at it. I need you to help me with this, son," he said to the Man of Music, jerking his head at the old man in the front seat. "Fifteen-minute stop, mister!" he said to the old man in a loud voice. "We gon' get you some fresh air!" The Man of Music squatted down by the old man, put his arm around his shoulder, and said, "Get ready, buddy, we gon' take a walk." The bus driver grabbed the old man under the arms and the Man of Music grabbed him by the feet. Out of respect for his dignity, the little lady looked the other way while they bent the old man around the front seat and headfirst out the door and set him up on a bench on the sidewalk looking down over the town. In the distance we could see Lake Despera looking dark and still, the cupola of the Chautauqua building gleaming in the sunlight, and the big old houses on Circle Drive. It was all so peaceful it seemed as if there were no people but us in Despera Springs that day. The Man of Music lit two cigarettes and held one of them up to the old man's face. His hands lay helpless in his lap, but he reached out his lips and plucked in the cigarette with a neat snap. He closed his eyes and smoked expertly and appreciatively, the whole bottom of his face wobbling with ecstasy. After a while the Man of Music pinched the cigarette away, flicked off the ash, then put it back into those reaching lips.

"Lucky Strike," said the Man of Music. "Can't go wrong." Then it seemed as if he couldn't be still. First he sat on the edge of the bench, smoking his cigarette and tapping his feet with his hands twitching between his knees. Then he stood up and walked halfway down to Lake Despera and back. He did a little shuffling dance in front of the old man, his cigarette between his teeth, his arms flopping loose at his sides. The little boy stood on the sidewalk and watched closely.

When the fifteen minutes were up and we all loaded back on the bus and headed west, the little old lady took out a big plastic bag and began unpacking a feast–slices of hummingbird cake, slabs of banana bread, cookies dredged in powdered sugar, sliced ham wrapped up in tinfoil, and a cardboard box of fried chicken.

"Y'all come on up and help yourselves," she said. "You know I can't walk on this moving bus." To me she whispered, "It's left over from the funeral of my brother-in-law's wife, but we won't tell them that." And to them she said, "What you can't eat, take home. It's all good food, there's not a thing in the world wrong with it."

The Man of Music sat on the edge of the seat by the old man and fed him little crumbles of pound cake, poking it into his smacking mouth with the tips of his fingers. The old man gummed each bit, dribbling crumbs down his chest, swallowed, and opened his mouth for more.

The lady made up about a dozen sandwiches out of biscuits and ham for the little boy. "You need to eat," she told him. "You don't know if your grandma will have supper for you in Pensacola."

"Lucky Strike," said the Man of Music. "I'm making up a song, y'all. I can feel it coming on; I believe it's gon' be about true love."

"By then Governor Wallace was getting used to me," the bus driver said. "And one day he said, 'You like me, boy, don't you?' 'Yessir, I do,'" I said. "'Well, I like you, too, boy, and when you grow up, I'm gon' send you to law school.'"

The little lady carefully spread a napkin out over her lap. "Mayhaws, plums, scuppernongs, she'd make jelly out of anything in season," she said. "Way more than anybody could eat. There was no reasoning with her when it came to jams and jellies."

"I wanted to go to law school," said the bus driver. "I was ambitious; I wanted to grow up to be president of the United States. But I did one thing wrong. I fell in love."

"Uh-uh, honey, don't," sang the Man of Music.

"My granny says there's a word for what my mama is, but she won't say that word," said the little boy.

"In fact you could say it was jams and jellies that killed her," said the little lady, nibbling delicately on a chicken wing, holding it wrapped up in a napkin to spare her short white gloves.

"Governor Wallace was a smart man," said the bus driver. "He said to me, 'Boy, this is puppy love. You gon' get married, tie yourself down with a passel of young-uns, and you can kiss law school good-bye.' He was right, too, I never made it to law school."

"She fell over dead at the stove, making jelly," said the little lady, "knocked the pot of mayhaw juice onto the floor at a full rolling boil and the jelly bag still dripping over the sink."

"Governor Wallace gave me a job, though," said the bus driver. "He hired me to be his driver. That's how I raised my kids, seventeen years driving the governor anywhere he wanted to go."

"What's your mama's name?" the Man of Music asked the little boy. "I'm gon' put her in my song."

"Now my brother-in-law is bad to drink," the little lady said, "and when he came in late that night and there she was on the kitchen floor laying in that red pool of mayhaw juice starting to jell and the lumpy jelly bag hanging over the sink, all he could think of was blood and hearts."

"One night we were riding along, just me and him," said the bus driver, "through some pine woods in south Alabama. It was dark. Nobody was talking. Then just out of nowhere he said, 'Boy, there's something about me you don't like. What is it?'"

"Her name's Alma, but they call her Sweetie," said the little boy.

"Oooh, baby," said the Man of Music. "True love! It's gon' be about a bus ride. Your mama ever ride the bus?"

"Well, that kind of put me on the spot," said the bus driver. "'Cause he was right. There was something I didn't like. But I just told the truth. I said, 'Well, Governor, you know, I ain't prejudice.' And he sat right there and said to me, 'Boy, I'll tell you something not many people know about me. I ain't prejudice either.'"

"My brother-in-law just couldn't get it out of his mind," said the little lady. "He'd go out on the porch, open up that freezer, that light would come on in that white freezer, and he'd just stand there and look in at all those Clorox jugs of plum juice and those gallon-size plastic bags of mayhaws she had stacked up in there, tears running down his face; all he could see was hearts and blood."

"You know," said the Man of Music, "I get around; I bet I'm gon' run into your mama one day."

"My daddy said she just couldn't be satisfied," said the little boy. "And that's why she left."

"I couldn't stand to see him suffering like that," said the little lady. "So the night before the funeral while he was asleep, I emptied out that freezer and made seventy-seven pints of jelly, stained up my hands so bad squeezing the bag I had to go out first thing in the morning and buy these short white gloves."

"She'll have a big pocketbook," said the little boy.

"Yeah," said the Man of Music. "I'll know her by that pocketbook."

"They call her Sweetie," said the little boy.

"I know that," said the Man of Music. "And when I see her, I'm gon' tell her I rode the bus with you. I'm gon' tell her how you helped me write this song about true love. I'm gon' tell her we sat here and ate a ham sandwich together. I'm gon' tell her you are a nice little boy. What else you want me to tell her?"

"Tell her I said hey."

We all just sat for a while, eating funeral food, thinking about true love and death and music and blood and hearts and mayhaw jelly, and watching the end of that bright afternoon. The little lady opened up her book of advice for living. "'Fear nothing,'" I read over her shoulder. "'Live without regrets.'" But soon it was too dark to read, and by the time we got to the outskirts of Pensacola, it was night. There was a lot of traffic, changing lanes and merging, and the bus driver had to concentrate on his driving. Even the Man of Music sat still, with his seat reared back, and the old man across from us had his eyes closed.

There was some confusion after the bus stopped at the big Greyhound station in Pensacola—bright lights suddenly came on inside the bus, and the bus driver sang out over the loudspeaker, "Pensacola, Florida!" The old man jerked awake in his seat and stared around with wild, startled eyes. The little lady started trying to give us all plastic bags of food, and the Man of Music got his guitar case wedged between the seats. A mean-faced woman with a grim, narrow mouth came bustling onto the bus, grabbed the little boy up by the forearm, and marched him down the aisle with her eyes downcast, saying impatiently, "Excuse me, excuse me," as we stepped out of her way.

"Grandma, see him?" The little boy turned back and pointed. "Grandma, see? He's a man of music. I helped him write a song about—"

But the woman snatched him down the steps, saying, "Now, I do not have time . . ."

A put-upon-looking young woman wearing tight blue jeans with her feet mashed into clear-plastic, high-heeled shoes came to meet my little lady. "You may be wondering—" the little lady started saying.

But the young woman was staring with horror at the boxes of jelly jars being unloaded from the luggage compartment of the bus, two teetering stacks of white boxes on the sidewalk, and more to come. She smacked her lips and flopped her arms at the little lady in a fit of irritation. "What in the world—I do not have room . . ."

The Man of Music took his guitar over to a group of young women who were lounging around on the orange plastic benches, clutching snagged blankets and dingy pillows, reading magazines and eating candy bars, waiting for the Atlanta bus. "Y'all ready for some music?" the Man of Music asked. "'Cause I'm here now." But not a single one even bothered to look up at him.

The last person to come off the bus was the old man. The bus driver and a tall, silent man each got under one arm and walked him off the bus, his feet flopping down the steps. They tried to set him up in a rickety wheelchair, but he landed crooked in the seat with his sweater rucked up under his arms, and the tall man and a stooped old woman pushed him on out of the bus station like that, without bothering to straighten him up.

Return to Sender

"MAMA, YOU CAN'T order things out of that catalog," said Emily. She was going through her mother's mail, and as usual, several envelopes were addressed to Sears Roebuck and Co. in her mother's shaky penmanship, stamped RETURN TO SENDER with the pointing hand.

"Luten had one of these American Beauty top buggies," said Mrs. Nash. She was looking at the ads for horse-drawn carriages in a Sears catalog reprinted from 1909. "'More than a hundred little special features in the manufacture go to make this a smoother, handsomer, more stylish, more lasting and better top buggy than could be had for twice the price.' That's absolutely true," she said, squinting at the grainy black-and-white illustration through a magnifying glass. "It was black, with stripes in a New York red. It had velvet carpet on the floor and a tufted leather seat."

Emily's sister, Lucille, thought they should throw out the Sears catalog. "It just encourages her," said Lucille. But Emily kept remembering what the woman had told them at the Alzheimer's seminar, that the old memories were the strongest, and if you could connect the old and the new, you might be able to open up pathways of communication. Emily sat down with her mother and pointed to the cover of the catalog. "Mama, look right here where it says 'A Treasured Replica from the Archives of History.' The catalog isn't real. It's a copy. You can't order things out of it."

"It is real," said Mrs. Nash. "Just look at this. I remember that deep roll on the seat and the nickel dash rail and the antirattlers; the ride was just as smooth."

"Mama," said Emily, but Mrs. Nash had turned to mantel clocks and statues of women and hunting dogs to set on top of them and wouldn't listen.

✦

The next morning Emily gave her daily report to her sister, Lucille, on the telephone. "She's ordering things out of the catalog," Emily said. "A horse-drawn buggy and some kind of big old britches."

"You need to throw out that catalog," said Lucille. "She's got to live in the real world, Emily, like the rest of us."

"Remember what the woman said about the old and the new and the pathways of communication?" said Emily. But Lucille was busy raising her illegitimate grandson and planning the town's big Victorian Christmas celebration and didn't have time to listen to Emily talk about pathways in their mother's brain. Emily heard a series of beeps from the telephone where Lucille had mashed her cheek against the buttons, then in the background "O Holy Night" and little Ned snuffling and whimpering.

"Emily, I'm cooking five meals for Mama, I'm feeding Ned, and I've got to get the music lined up for downtown, the soundman is coming tomorrow. Don't start talking to me about grass."

Ever since they had attended the Alzheimer's seminar Emily had been imagining her mother's mind like a green meadow with a blue sky overhead, and something like a bush hog cutting graceful, curving swaths through the tall, soft grass. Emily had always been that way, her thoughts would just stick on one useless topic, like grass, for days at a time. There hadn't been a name for it, just a range of adjectives, from "delicate" to "no-count," until last year Lucille had decided that Emily had attention deficit disorder, gotten her a prescription for Ritalin, and given her her first job, sewing the Victorian strollers' costumes for the downtown Christmas celebration.

"She is an extremely capable seamstress," Lucille had insisted when the wardrobe chairman had said, stretching her eyes wide, "Emily?" And sure enough, on just three little pills a day, Emily had completed forty of the costumes. They hung from the picture molding all around the living room—tailcoats, weskits, skirts with bustles, and jackets with leg-of-mutton sleeves.

"Horse," said the baby, pointing with a gummy finger. He was sitting in Mrs. Nash's lap looking at the harness in the Sears catalog while Emily sewed piping in a bodice seam and Lucille washed a load of clothes and stacked up frozen food in the top of the refrigerator.

"That is the martingale and those are the traces," said Mrs. Nash. "That strap runs through a loop right here and fastens to the shaft."

"Horse," said the baby.

"Emily, look here," called Lucille. "This food is numbered. You fix one first, then two; when you get down to five, I'll come back, see this?"

"Horse," said the baby.

"Who is this baby?" said Mrs. Nash. "Whose little baby is this?"

"Come on, Ned," said Lucille, snatching him up and ratcheting him up a notch on her hip. "These look good, Emily," she said, counting silently and fingering the hood of a scarlet cape. "Forty, and you've only got two weeks. Did you take your pill today?" Then the front door scraped and the screen door banged and Lucille was gone, with the little baby reaching back over her shoulder calling, "Horse, horse."

✦

"I've got to rearrange the musicians; they've got the Greasy String Band too close to the Baptist-church handbell choir, and I've got to reschedule the live Nativity because the first Baby Jesus has to be a mouse in ''Twas the Night before Christmas.' Emily, I won't be able to come tomorrow. So remember–five dresses to go, and throw out that catalog."

"I think you need to tell her about Ned," said Emily.

"She doesn't know 1909 from 1999, she doesn't need to know about Ned," said Lucille.

It had all started with body piercing, Lucille was convinced; her little girl, Cindy, only fourteen years old, coming home one night with a ring through her eyebrow, and soon after that the boy with the hank of hair and the spiderweb tattooed on his elbow and no expression in his eyes, and then without so much as a by-your-leave, this phlegmatic little lump of a baby plopped down in the middle of it all. "Don't you even think?" Lucille had shouted. But Cindy had just looked at her with the same bland look the baby had and tapped the gold stud in her tongue against the side of her back teeth.

In the end there was nothing Lucille could do but take on the little baby, feed him and keep him clean, and try to teach him things. He was a slow learner; so far he only knew one word, *horse*, from his great-grandmother's Sears catalog. He never said *Mama*, which everyone expects to hear first, and he seemed to be confused about his own name, Denorrio; but no one could blame him for that, since Lucille called him Ned.

"Denorrio!" said Lucille. "They string together a bunch of consonants and vowels and call it a name. Gibberish names, they pluck them out of thin air, just like these babies. Ned!" she said one day, putting her face right down in front of the baby, who was peacefully gnawing on his little fist. "What's wrong with plain old Ned?"

Now, two days left—forty-seven costumes completed. Emily felt satisfied and proud just looking at them: the ten wool blends with braid trim, the fifteen corduroy (the nap had been hard to handle), the seven plaid skirts with piping, and a row of plush capes with gracefully draping hoods. Now, with the end in sight she had abandoned the simple Folkways patterns they had given her and begun to copy a dress from the old Sears catalog, with a high-standing collar, a square yoke in front, and shoulder capes. She had made it twice, once in a royal blue, and now she was almost finished with her favorite, a lovely fawn corduroy with double feather stitching around the hem. Secretly, at the beginning of the week, she had left off taking the little pills, and now, Thursday, the twitchy, jumpy feeling was almost gone and she could just sit and sew, enjoying the weight of the skirt in her lap, the soft hand of the fabric, and the small sounds in the room—the tiny *tap-tap* of the needle against her thimble, the rustle of the catalog pages, and her mother whispering the names of horse-drawn conveyances: runabout, cabriolet, surrey, phaeton. Through the ripply, old glass of the tall windows the green of the grass and bushes looked smeary and distant, and Emily could almost forget it was just an overgrown yard on

Dawson Street and imagine a meadow with wide paths in graceful curves.

Then all at once up the walkway came Lucille, dragging an ice chest on wheels and a canvas bag of clean sheets. She set Ned down in Mrs. Nash's lap and grabbed up the lovely fawn corduroy skirt, snatching the thread out of the needle.

"Horse, horse," said Ned.

". . . that little top buggy, and the prettiest little brown-and-white pony you ever saw, Apple Jack was his name," said Mrs. Nash.

"Emily, what are you thinking?" said Lucille. "You can't be hand-sewing feather stitching around three yards of hem with less than forty-eight hours to go, can't you see that? It won't show from a distance anyway, you should be hot-gluing this braid on here."

"Horse," said Ned.

"Oh, Emily!" said Lucille. "Look at this, you can't let Mama sit on the upholstered furniture, you have to take her to the bathroom, you know she won't go by herself and, Lord, Ned wet, too, and we don't even know who peed on who!"

"Whom," whispered Emily.

"Don't *whom* me!" said Lucille. "Take this baby. Mama, get up, stand on this towel; hold on to the back of this chair. Here I am, in the middle of a hot flash, trying to get my forty-five-year-old sister her first paying job, thawing out my little girl's breast milk in the microwave, and changing the diaper on my mama, all at the same time. There is no God in this world, Emily, if there was he'd be down here screwing the lid on this sippy cup."

In Emily's lap Ned squirmed and whimpered and beat his arms up and down. Emily held him by his little shoulders. The back of his head smelled like vanilla wafers. "Look," she whispered. But out the window the grassy meadow with its graceful paths was gone, and all Emily could think about was the plastic model of the human brain from the Alzheimer's seminar, with its anxious gray color, its worried-looking furrows, and a high-gloss finish making it look wet and slimy.

✦

December 10, 1999. In the early dusk, yellow-striped sawhorses were put across both ends of Broad and Jackson streets, closing off six blocks to automobile traffic. At six thirty a couple of Jersey cows, a little donkey, and some sheep and goats were unloaded from a horse trailer and tethered with a bale of hay in the middle of the vacant lot where the picture show used to be, and a rooster was tied by one leg to the palmetto-frond roof of the little two-by-four stable for the live Nativity. At first dark the little twinkling lights on the Bradford pear trees were turned on, and the newly reinstalled 1890 streetlamps were lit for the first time, to a cheering ovation. On the corner of Jackson and Broad, the Greasy String Band started up with "Old Joe Clark," and in front of the bookstore the handbell choir chimed out "Oh Come All Ye Faithful." Smells of cooking spread out from the parking lot of Toscoga Seed, where the Griffin brothers were barbecuing beef ribs, and there was the creak of harness and the *cloppety-clop* of horse hooves on the brick street as the carriage rides started up. The Victorian strollers, magnificent in Emily's costumes, mingled with the crowd, mincing along in their bustled skirts and their button-up shoes.

The Victorian downtown Christmas celebration was perfect except for the two unfinished dresses, and Lucille had even managed to fix that with a couple of old prom dresses from Goodwill, a box of safety pins, and some big scarves.

Emily had to stay at home. "You can't leave her," Lucille had said, "even for a minute. She'll wander off and get lost. And you'll have to keep Ned, too, because Cindy is a Victorian stroller."

But even that far down Dawson Street, Emily could hear the brass band from the high school, and from the porch she could see a golden glow in the sky from downtown. Who would be wearing the fawn corduroy dress with the half-finished feather stitching? she wondered. Would they wear the snoods on the capes up or down? Ned was sound asleep in his portable crib in the living room, and Mrs. Nash was dozing in the rocking chair. If she went straight up Dawson and cut through the Flemings' backyard, it would only take two minutes, Emily thought. She would just stand for a little while behind Mr. Zalumis's peanut cart, where Lucille would never see her.

She was out of breath when she got there, and she stood for a minute in the shadow of the awning on the peanut cart, huffing and puffing. The town looked so different with no cars on the streets, and beautiful—the twinkling lights shining through the red leaves on the trees, and the steady golden glow of the streetlamps highlighting the architectural details of the tall, old storefronts, their corbeled tops and bay windows silhouetted against an indigo sky. The whole town was like one of those charming stereopticon scenes described in the old Sears catalog.

There! Emily saw a handsome, dark-haired woman wearing the sage-green wool dress where she had had to miter in a length of piping in the bodice seam, and a teenaged girl in the royal blue corduroy; she had had to sew in tissue paper to keep the fabric from crawling on that one. She was glad to see the seams lying flat and smooth, the skirts swaying gracefully, and the wide ribbon borders on the hems unfurling so beautifully around the folds. She saw Ned's mother, Cindy, wearing the brown velveteen cape, smiling and laughing and feeding her boyfriend a piece of sweet-potato pie. Even with her bad ways she had given in to the spirit of Victorian Christmas and covered up the Celtic tattoo on her arm with a long-sleeved white shirt. Then suddenly there was Lucille standing in the middle of Broad Street talking on a cell phone. Emily ducked behind Mr. Zalumis. Lucille stood still with her head down, listening.

"That can't be," she said into the telephone. "There are no carriages with tops. And they don't go down Dawson; they go from Broad to Jackson, then left on Remington, and come back up Monroe. I told them to pause at the Culpepper-Bailey house if they get ahead of time so they don't pile up in front of the library, but there would never be a reason for them to go down Dawson."

"That's a hard-driving woman," said Mr. Zalumis, the peanut man.

"She's my sister," whispered Emily.

"Hmm," said Mr. Zalumis, and he handed her a little bag of candied peanuts. Mr. Zalumis had inherited the peanut stand thirty years ago from his father, Old Mr. Zalumis, and the secret recipe for peanut brittle, containing a certain amount of coconut. Now Mr. Zalumis himself was old, with tangled eyebrows and a prickly, white stubble. He wore little round wire spectacles, a bowler hat, and red suspenders holding his pants up too high. But it wasn't a costume; Mr. Zalumis just always dressed like that.

"She tried to give me a monkey," Mr. Zalumis said. "The monkey had a little red suit and a little red hat with a gold band. He had wore all the hair off his tail. 'Hell, lady,' I told her, 'I don't want no damn monkey.' That woman thinks she can run this whole town."

They watched Lucille click the telephone off and slide it into a little holster on her belt and head off down the street.

"She's wrong about that buggy, though," said Mr. Zalumis. "I saw that buggy going down Dawson. Pretty thing, wheels just as high, and a little bow top, stretched tight, and a little brown-and-white prancy pony."

Emily spat out a peanut. "Was it black? Did it have red stripes?"

"Coal black," said Mr. Zalumis. "Shiny red stripes. Brand-new, not a scratch on it."

Back at home the front door was wide open. Mrs. Nash wasn't in her chair, and Ned was awake, standing up in his crib in his droopy drawers, calling, "Horse! Horse!" Emily picked him up and walked through the rooms of the house, trying to think. It was all her fault. She had never thrown out the Sears catalog. But there wasn't anything she could do about it now, she thought, with Lucille in the middle of Victorian Christmas. She might as well just sit down on the back steps for a while, with her cheek against the back of Ned's head, and listen to the brass band.

In the red-clay dirt of Snodgrass Alley she could see the horse tracks going down the middle of the road, and the tracks of the narrow wheels on each side, dug deep. For a while the tracks veered from side to side in graceful curves, as if the horse had felt frisky with such a light load, seeing the road stretching out so long and straight in front of him, but after a block or two the tracks straightened out and ran on down the road, steady and true, and out of sight.

Lonesome Without You

THE BOY'S NAME was Mel. Ever since his mother had died of breast cancer a year ago, he had lived with his grandmother, who thought up worthwhile projects for him such as charting rainfall amounts and raising rabbits for meat—"to keep his mind off it," she said. But lately Mel had been spending most of his spare time sitting at the picnic table down at the new Citgo Gas Station and Cigarette Outlet, watching women vacuum out their cars.

When his mother had died, the counselor had given his grandmother a little book to read about grief, dividing it up into five stages, and she didn't see how hanging around down at the gas station fit into a stage of grief. "You're loitering!" she said.

Mel wasn't sure what *loitering* meant, but he didn't like the sound of it. It seemed like it must have something to do with the way he sometimes felt about certain women and the vacuum cleaner, when they would go down under the backseat with it, or crawl around in the backs of the station wagons and *wuuhmp!*—that satisfying sound when the vacuum would suck up a candy wrapper or the cellophane off a cigarette pack.

In fact, at certain moments at the Citgo, Mel would feel so happy he could hardly believe it—the flap of the little plastic flags; the angle of the morning sun; a whiff of gasoline and hot dogs; Nancy, the itinerant gardener, who was always nice to him, digging in the corner flower bed; and Gabby broadcasting *Country Like It Used to Be* on the radio, saying, "And now a new hour begins on 93.3—ten a.m."

That was the best part, when the nurse would drive in to fill up and vacuum out her car. Every Saturday morning at ten, he could count on it. First she would take out the floor mats, shake them out, and rub them on the grass. Then she would take everything out of the car and line it all up in neat, straight rows along the curb—a Georgia atlas and gazetteer, a pair of sneakers, a blue-and-white ice chest. She would open all the car doors and dig in a little red purse for the quarters. Then the roar of the vacuum would drown out the country music. Mel loved the graceful way she shook out the loops in the hose and stepped over it so carefully in her white shoes. She vacuumed around the doorframe, a place most people missed, and she always vacuumed the whole car on two quarters.

The nurse was never in a hurry, and sometimes she would sit down at the picnic table beside the little flower bed and talk to Nancy. Mel kept weekly records about the nurse in a black notebook—"Arrival and Departure Times," "Contents of Car," "No. of Gallons and Purchase Price of Gas"—he learned from observation. But the list he kept in the back of the notebook, "Miscl. Facts of Interest," he got from eavesdropping. Her birthday was in June, her sister raised prizewinning goldfish, she had once owned a dog named Happy who had a skin problem.

One Saturday in January the nurse asked Nancy, "How do you root a rose? This old lady I'm nursing has a red rose in her backyard, in full bloom since Christmas."

"You have to wait till spring," said Nancy.

"This old lady won't last that long," said the nurse.

"Red rose, blooms all year," Mel wrote in his notebook.

On a February Saturday when Nancy was putting in some cool-weather plants for spring, the nurse sat down by a flat of lamb's ears on the picnic table. "I never saw a gray plant," she said, feeling the soft, floppy leaves.

"*Stachys,*" said Nancy. "It can't take the heat though."

"I used to have a boyfriend whose earlobes felt just like this. I think his name was Bob."

"Bob," Mel wrote in his black notebook, and he thought about it a long time—Bob.

Another Saturday, when the vacuum shut off, the nurse didn't hang up the hose right away, but stood there listening to *Country Like It Used to Be* on the radio, Keith Whitley singing "I'm Lonesome Without You."

"This is my favorite song," the nurse said to Nancy. "Listen to this banjo part right here." Nancy stopped digging and they stood there, Nancy leaning on her shovel and the nurse dangling the pleated hose. They listened to the end of the song: "But if you should ever change your mind, dear, remember me, I'll be around."

"That's sad," said Nancy. "That old boy's just fooling himself, 'cause you know she ain't coming back."

Then the song was over, the nurse started coiling up the hose, and an advertisement came on the radio for an herbal breast-enlargement treatment. *Breast* was another of those terrible words like *loiter* that seemed to mean way too much. Mel felt his face burning.

"If you are like many women, you may not be happy with the way your breasts look and feel," said the announcer in a loud, penetrating voice. Suddenly Mel couldn't stand it. He stood up and stammered, "You—you—you don't know that for sure! She might not be gone forever! She *might* come back!" The nurse stared at him, beginning to smile, and Nancy grabbed him and hugged him tight. She smelled like pine straw. "You're cute," she said. "You just keep on thinking that way, sweetie."

"I know you from somewhere," said the nurse.

"Favorite Song," he wrote in his notebook, "Lonesome Without You.'"

On a Saturday in early March the nurse was almost ten minutes late. She filled up with gas, 14.54 gallons, but on this day she didn't vacuum out the car.

"Dying is hard work," she said. "I am exhausted." She lay down on the bench of the picnic table and scratched around in her hair with all her fingers.

Nancy brushed off her hands and rooted around in the bottom of her pocketbook for quarters. "Mel, go get us a Cocola, we could all use a break."

When he got back, they were sitting across from each other with their elbows on the table talking about colors. "Sometimes when I'm this tired, I close my eyes and I just see blue," said the nurse. She closed her eyes. "It looks like I'm on a Caribbean cruise." Her mouth took on a different look, like a sleeping baby's mouth, as if with her eyes closed, it didn't know what it was doing. Mel stared at her, memorizing little things he would write down later, how her eyelashes lay against her cheek, how a piece of hair curled in front of her ear.

"Nothing but sky and water," she said, "and it's all my favorite color—blue." Over by the ice machine a woman scratched off a lottery ticket. A jaybird lit in the chased tree. This is important, thought Mel.

✦

"Rabbit manure is the best fertilizer in the world," said his grandmother. She was raking around under the rabbit hutch while Mel tacked wire on a new pen. His grandmother was always trying to teach him that life is a cycle, that nothing ever really ends, that it all just goes around and around and around—and rabbit manure was the proof of it.

"After we get these rabbits in the freezer," she said, "we'll take this rabbit manure, spread it around the rosebush, and step back! That rosebush will jump up out of the ground. Life just takes on a new form."

Mel saw this as an opportunity. "What's a red rose that blooms in December?"

"Louis Philippe," said his grandmother. "Now why in the world do you want to know a thing like that?"

"Somebody at the Citgo wants to know."

"Citgo? Citgo? Have you been loitering down there at that Citgo?"

✦

On the next Saturday morning as Mel sat at the picnic table with his notebook watching Nancy prune the chased tree, his grandmother pulled up by the gas pump. She sat in the car for a long time, looking around like a private eye. Then she got out.

"Is this boy bothering you?" she asked Nancy. "Is he making you nervous with all that loitering? Look on the door," she said to Mel, and she read out loud, "No Loitering."

All he could think of was how he did not want the nurse to drive up right then, and all he could see was Nancy standing in the flower bed staring at his grandmother, and all he could feel was his grandmother's fingers digging into his arm, and all he could hear was that terrible word *loiter loiter loiter;* and something else, a remembered sound that came back sometimes—his mother's long, sucking, ratchety breaths, coming again and again, strangled and desperate, until he had to cover up his ears.

But then Nancy came up to them, reaching out a hand. "Please don't think that," she said. "He's not loitering, he keeps me company and helps me with the flower bed."

After that day, to make it the truth, Nancy put Mel to work spreading mulch. When the nurse finished vacuuming the next Saturday, Nancy said, "My new helper."

The nurse came over and sat down at the picnic table. "I wish I had a little flower garden like that."

"Why can't you?" said Nancy. "Everybody should be able to have some kind of little garden."

"I live in a third-floor apartment." The nurse sat backward on the bench and leaned against the table. "Just a little square of ground, in a quiet place, where I could go and sit sometimes."

The next Saturdays they planted the summer garden—nasturtiums, marigolds, and zinnias. Nancy taught Mel names—rattlesnake root, butterfly ginger, false dragonhead; and she told him what would happen in the summer and then in the fall. "Your best gardening is always in the future," she said. Sometimes there would be some plants left over in the flat and Nancy would give them to him, their roots wrapped in wet newspaper: "You take these home to your grandmother."

✦

It was time to separate the rabbits. They were going by a book, *Raising Rabbits for Fun and Profit*. "You will find great satisfaction in efficiency," said Mel's grandmother, grabbing the big, old buck rabbit and wrestling him through the little swinging door of the next pen.

Soon the female rabbit began lining the box with fur, and one day the nest was heaving with little pink squirmers. "See that?" said his grandmother. "Life marches on."

✦

Then it was summer, and the marigolds and zinnias spread and shaded out the weeds. There was plenty of rain and for a while there was nothing to do in the flower bed at the Citgo, and Nancy only came every other Saturday to pick up trash. Even as early as ten it was too hot to sit at the picnic table and visit, so the nurse just waved from the vacuum machine. "Where's your helper?" she called.

"Off somewhere growing up I guess," said Nancy.

"Uh-oh."

The baby rabbits grew a little soft, white down, and their eyes opened. “This is a good mama rabbit,” said Mel’s grandmother. “Look how fat they are.”

But all Mel wanted to do was study the lists in his black notebook and make his plans. He bought chart paper, one inch equals a foot, and he drew it over and over until he got it the way he wanted—a flower garden with a neat edge, straight rows, a smooth path, and a little place to sit. When he got it right, he colored it in with crayons, gray-blue for the border of lamb’s ears. “Bob,” he said to himself. “Bob.”

Then the real work started. It was hot and there was a lot of walking and hauling—blue bottles from the recycle center, bags of rabbit manure, the trays of little plants, and worst of all the bag of Sakrete. The ground was as hard as a rock—nothing ever got dug there but graves. Mel had to wait until a soaking rain before he could get a spade in it to dig out the centipede grass. He cut his finger breaking up the bottles, he stuck himself on the prickles of the rosebush, and one day he got into a wasp nest. There were unforeseen difficulties: He mixed the Sakrete too watery in his first batch, before he learned better, and the blue apostrophe in *I’m* sank out of sight. He had to shift the path over a foot from his plan; an old Stringer great-grandfather's grave marker would have stuck up between *lonesome* and *without*. And he had to plant a taller variety of marigolds to hide his mother's marker. It stuck up too high and looked too shiny. But finally he took an aluminum lawn chair out there and set it up on a little circle he had paved for it at the head of the path between the Louis Philippe rosebushes. He sat down with his elbows on his knees. It felt just right.

"Your best gardening is always in the future," Nancy had said, and finally, in early fall, it seemed as if the future was here. Even the weeds in the roadside ditches looked like a garden—foamy goldenrod and blue ageratum, nodding heads of summer-farewell and yellow spires of crotalaria, all twined around with the twinkling red of cardinal vine—everything putting on a last show before the frost.

◆

"At eight weeks of age the rabbits should weigh between four and five pounds and are ready to harvest," Mel's grandmother read in *Raising Rabbits for Fun and Profit*. "Now this won't be bad at all," she said to Mel. "They won't suffer."

But it was a Saturday morning, and while his grandmother was rummaging around in the kitchen drawer looking for gallon-size freezer bags, Mel sneaked off to the Citgo.

"Well, look at you!" said Nancy. "I bet you've grown four inches!"

"Where's your black book?" asked the nurse.

"I want to show you something," said Mel.

"Well, sure," said Nancy.

"Right now?" said the nurse.

"What is it?" said Nancy.

"We have to drive there," said Mel.

"How far?" said the nurse.

The graveyard was way down 93 from the Citgo, past Mel's house, then left on the Stringer Road, across from the cornfield at the Gainey Crossing. They rode in Nancy's truck, the nurse and Nancy in the front, and Mel in the back with the shovels and rakes and bales of pine straw and plastic pots, calling out to Nancy where to turn. It was an old graveyard, mostly Gaineys and Mel's family, the Stringers. Years ago there had been a fence around it, and a fancy gate with wrought-iron lilies and leaves, but now most of the fence was gone, and two big, old live-oak trees had crumpled the gate. In the front of the graveyard there was a chipped-up urn lying on its side, and a few weather-beaten angels and lumpish lambs, and old Gainey grave markers every which way like snaggleteeth. But in the Stringer plot, a low granite wall framed in a little square of ground, and you couldn't see the graves for the flowers—mounds of golden lion's beard, sweeps of pink and white chrysanthemums, nodding silvery heads of summer-farewell, and yellow swamp daisies flopping over the edge. Right down the middle of it, bordered with lamb's ears, ran a narrow paved path, with chips and shards of blue bottle glass set in the concrete to spell out the words I'M LONESOME WITHOUT YOU, and at the end, between two red rosebushes, an aluminum chair.

It was hard to know what to say about it, and they just stood there staring. The nurse was the first to speak. "Now isn't this the prettiest thing. Your mama was lucky to have had a boy who loved her enough to do all this."

He had thought she would understand after all those Saturdays, but in the end Nancy was the one who remembered the blue of the Caribbean cruise, Bob's ears, the banjo solo, the little quiet place to sit. Nancy grabbed Mel and hugged him around the head so he couldn't hear all that was said. "He did it for you!" she said to the nurse in a whisper.

"Me!" said the nurse. "What for?"

Mel pulled loose and tried to talk. "You were the one," he said. "You came that night, when she was breathing like that, you were the one who stopped her suffering."

The nurse sat down in the chair. Just as he had planned, the little blue-glass-mosaic banjo he had set into the concrete fit exactly between her feet.

But she didn't seem happy about it. "That wasn't me, honey," she said. "It was just her time. That wasn't me, that was Sister Morphine that stopped her suffering." She stood up and brushed herself off as if there might have been trash in the chair. "I'm no angel, I'm just a hospice nurse!"

When they got back to the Citgo, a man was mad because the nurse had left her car blocking the vacuum, and while she tried to explain—"I didn't know we'd be gone that long"—Nancy sat Mel down on the picnic bench with his back to the nurse and squatted down in front of him with her hands on his knees.

"She's used to doing for other people," Nancy said. "She's not used to having other people do for her. She's not ungrateful, she just wasn't ready for such a thing. It took her by surprise."

But Mel couldn't listen to all that, and on the way home he started crying. He cried and cried just like a baby. He couldn't stop. At first his grandmother thought it was the rabbits and went on and on about never-ending cycles, but when he still didn't stop after supper and way on past bedtime, she decided it must be one of those stages of grief she had read about. "Well, finally!" she said.

And she was right in a way. Life did just march on and on. The first freeze came in about a week, and that was the end of the garden. Over the winter the concrete path cracked into pieces—Mel hadn't known how thick to make it. The polished side of his mother's marker with her name and the dates lost some of its shine, and lichen sprouted on the rough backside, so it started to blend in with all the other Stringers and Gaineys. Centipede grass is an aggressive spreader, and it sent out runners across the walkway until by August you could only see a few little chips of the blue here and there, shining through the grass, that used to say I'M LONESOME WITHOUT YOU.

The Garden

A Garden is a lovesome thing, God wot!
Rose plot,
Fringed pool,
Ferned grot—
The veriest school
Of peace; and yet the fool
Contends that God is not—
Not God! in gardens! when the eve is cool?
Nay, but I have a sign:
'Tis very sure God walks in mine.

CLINK, CLUNK, CLINK. Day after day that summer they could hear the little taps of the chisel as Nana carved those words into a slab of marble out in the new garden she was making on the side of the house. By

August the carving was done, little, wobbly letters with mismatched serifs crawling across the pink marble slab.

That winter she planted two little tea-olive trees at the entrance to the garden, and the rose plot from the poem—Lady Banksia, Dainty Bess, Cecil Brunner, and Seven Sisters around a bronze sundial.

The next summer was rainy, but she dug a round hole in the mud and planted pickerelweed around the edge, and that was the fringed pool.

The next spring, her skills in cement honed by the work she had done the year before lining the pool in the drizzling rain, she tackled the ferned grot and ended up in September with a slumping concrete dome with arched openings on four sides, studded with broken conch shells she'd picked up at the Gulf. "Like fossils from an ancient seabed," she told them intently, brushing the sand from her fingers in little twiddling motions.

The ferns began to thicken and spread, the roses bloomed, and the tea-olive trees were shoulder high. Nana laid little flagstone paths in artistic curves connecting the different features of the garden, bordered with Ophiopogon, and organized garden tea parties for her granddaughters. She dressed them up in white lawn and black stockings and tried to get them to assume graceful poses on the sloping concrete benches in the ferned grot, teacup in one hand, saucer in the other. But mosquitoes swarmed out of the fringed pool, the black wool stockings were prickly and tight, and they didn't like hot tea.

"My God, woman," their grandfather roared down from the house. "What the hell is a grot?"

Then the tea party was over, cups hastily set down with relief, mosquito bites scratched at last, and one granddaughter poked her sister and whispered, "God wot!" With a chorus of giggles the granddaughters trooped back to the house, ignoring the graceful curving path and stomping over the Ophiopogon border. And Nana, in tears, was left to gather up the pieces of a broken cup.

Years went by; the tea-olive trees grew up and formed a canopy over the garden entrance, and the ferns took off and spread into the bog behind the garden formed by the leaky pool. In the 1940s the roof collapsed on the grot and it actually took on the look of some kind of ruin. Nana became more and more a figure of fun to her family as she aged. "God wot" evolved in the family linguistics into an expletive, and surrounded as she was by irreverent loved ones, Nana's sanity began to ebb. She was always brushing imaginary grains of sand off her fingers, and she thought that flowers were in bloom out of season.

"Oh, dearest!" she would gush on a dreary January afternoon, gesturing with twiddling fingers to the bleak, stubbly lawn, her eyes filling with tears. "Oh, dearest . . . the lilies!"

"God wot, woman!" her husband would growl, glaring at her from under his bushy eyebrows. "Can't you see it's the dead of winter? Ain't no lilies blooming out of that cold ground!"

In the 1950s the garden took over its own management. The more delicate Cecil Brunner and Dainty Bess succumbed to black spot, but the Seven Sisters grew into a mat over the sundial and the Lady Banksia climbed out of the garden and up into the tops of the pine trees. The ferns choked out the pickerelweed, and a race of giant black-and-red grasshoppers bred in the Ophiopogon borders.

Eva, one of the tea-drinking granddaughters, had inherited her grandmother's interest in botany, without the sentiment, and made a serious study of several species of indigenous rice. One summer Eva dug out the ferns that had taken over the half-acre bog behind the pool and planted rows of little rice plants there. It was a constant struggle to keep the ferns from taking back the bog, but in one year the rice grew to towering clumps. In the fall Eva gathered a bushel of it, shaking the grains out of the drooping heads. But she found it almost impossible to separate the grain from the husk. The winnowing method she set up on the porch with screen wire and a fan wasn't up to it. The husk, with its sharp, little backward-facing barbs clung tenaciously to the grain, and it needed many picking fingers to do the job. But Eva's children were no more interested in hulling rice than Eva herself had been at their age in Victorian tea parties, and the rice clumps went unharvested in the bog behind the garden, reseeding themselves year after year.

In the fall of 1968, Eva's son Louis went off to college and came home for his spring break with a new enthusiasm for gardening and many questions for Eva about the pH scale and dolomite lime. He spent days behind the garden, putting in drains and digging manures into the old rice field. On a hot afternoon in early September he took Eva for a walk through the old overgrown garden.

"I want to show you something," he told her.

They stopped behind the rubble-strewn grot, and Eva looked out over what used to be her rice plantation. "What is that?" she said. "Palmate leaves, edges dentate—it reminds me of rose of Sharon, but this square stem, like a mint. An odd smell for a plant, and these dense, gummy flower clusters. What are you growing here, Louis?"

"It's not rose of Sharon." Then Louis showed her his drying racks in the grot, and together they snipped off several bristling bundles of flowers. They sat on a bench near the roses and Louis rolled a thin, little yellow cigarette.

"This is against the law," said Eva, squinting her eyes and taking a little puff. Still, she thought, remembering the backward-facing barbs on every grain of rice, how could a thing be wicked when it was so easy to harvest? She lay back on the bench and closed her eyes. Little red pinpoints of light spread and burst into sparkles.

"God wot!" said Eva.

"Yeah," said Louis.

The summer day seemed to swell and ebb.

"There's a bronze sundial under those Seven Sisters," said Eva.

"Yeah," said Louis.

"I broke a teacup here once."

"Yeah."

The next afternoon a little propeller airplane flew low over the house, dipping and circling. That night Eva and Louis pulled up every one of the plants and threw them over the fence to the cows. All night there was that rhythmic munch, munch, munch, and when the airplane came back in the morning, nothing was left but a few straggling rice plants, starved for sunlight, and three sweet-faced Jersey cows snuffling their wet noses against the fence.

In the 1970s, Louis's sister Belle rode the bus out to California and married a poet. But she grew homesick, and she lured her husband back across the continent with poetical descriptions of Gulf breezes and the green evening mists in her great-grandmother's old garden. They planted a little eucalyptus tree behind the roses, a memento of California, Belle went to work in the family feed mill, and Eva cleared out a space for the California poet in a back room where old guns had been stored. But the damp and heat didn't agree with him, and no one understood his work.

"Nice-looking young fellow Belle brought back from California."

"Calls himself a poet."

"That's a real poetical family out there. I remember old Miss Anna carving out that poem, something about a garden."

"Sure did, chipped every letter out of a slab of marble she got down at the monument shop. Took her a whole summer."

"This California boy, though, he writes his on paper. Uses a typewriter I believe."

"Yeah, well, that ain't quite the same thing, now is it?"

When the poet broke out in prickly heat rash at the end of his second August, it was the last straw, and he packed his typewriter up and headed back out West. The eucalyptus tree, however, got its roots down into the septic-tank drainfield, and within three years it was towering over the garden, shedding great ragged slabs of bark in the fringed pool and breaking Belle's heart with the clean, sharp smell of her California love.

In the 1980s, people all over the country stopped eating eggs and beef because of the cholesterol scare, and the feed mill shut down. The mysterious tapping sounds they had been attributing to ghosts in the attic turned out to be drops of rainwater leaking through the roof and hitting the ceiling, and the plumbing backed up because the roots of the eucalyptus tree had clogged up the antique red-clay pipes that formed the septic-tank drainfield. The roofer came down out of the attic shaking his head, and the plumber came up from behind the garden saying, "Uh, uh, uh."

In 1987, Eva sold the house to a hotel-and-restaurant corporation. Within three months it was replumbed, rewired, reroofed, and repainted. A bulldozer leveled the grot and filled in the rice bog. In one day a team of professional gardeners hacked through the tangle of roses and ferns with Weed Eaters and chain saws until they came down to the old winding paths, the sundial, and the poem on its marble slab. They trimmed the opening under the tea-olive trees into a neat arch, they replaced the rampant Lady Banksia and Seven Sisters with modern, controllable roses, they patched the pool and installed a recirculating filter pump with a spray fountain and a bronze nymph, and they edged the Ophiopogon borders. In the ferns, where the grot had been, they put a teak Chinese Chippendale-style bench with a potted topiary-tree rosemary at each end.

In 1990, to commemorate its opening as a country inn, the house and its garden were featured on the cover of *Leisure South* magazine. In April, when the roses came into bloom, the magazine editor and a photographer came down from Atlanta. The editor was feeling weary of her job—the endless articles she would write in the magazine's relentlessly jaunty style about redecorating family rooms and putting up redwood fences. The photographer was feeling bitter. On the long drive from the airport he showed her a photograph he had taken at a New Year's celebration in Chinle, Arizona—an old man and an old woman dancing, their eyes closed, both his big, lumpy hands clasped behind her fat, bulging back. In the background glittery things shimmered out of the blackness.

"This is my *Moonrise over Hernandez,*" he said.

They stood for a minute in the shade of the two tea-olive trees and looked into the sunny garden.

"And here I am at another goddamned garden, another goddamned dewdrop on another goddamned rose, more of that goddamned green murk in the background." He stepped out into the sunlight and went to work, not quite focusing on a full-blown Tropicana rose, catching a rainbow in the spray behind the nymph, zooming in on a tiger swallowtail on a potted red geranium.

"What's this?" she said. "It might be a gravestone." She ran her fingers along the eroded lines of spidery letters. "We could do one of those rubbings," she said, squinting to read the words. "Something about a garden, God something, rose something. Here it says when something is cool, eve, 'when the eve is cool.'"

But it was hot in the sun on that April day, and she sat down on the teak bench in the shade and thought up titles for articles she might write: "Chintz Transforms a Foyer," "Lighten That Hedge with Old-Fashioned Elaeagnus!"

She lay back on the bench and closed her eyes. She could hear the clicks and whirrings of his camera like little birdsongs. Through her eyelids she could see shifting patterns of sun and shade.

"Imagine," she said, "this garden being here, unchanged, all these years."

"Yep," he said, stuffing rolls of film into the pockets of his vest. "Well, that's what we like about the South."

"Still, let's just sit here a minute, in the shade, in this peaceful place."

Nothing with Strings

LOUISE AND HER sister, Lily, were standing in the middle of the parking lot of a Super Wal-Mart in Despera Springs, Florida, trying to decide where to sprinkle their mother's ashes. They had driven for hours across the Panhandle to get here, with the ashes in a gold-toned plastic urn on the backseat, but now nothing seemed right. They kept remembering the stories their mother had told them all their lives of her Despera Springs childhood: the monkey who died in a watermelon rind; the mysterious stranger who walked around behind a blue mule and was never seen again; the brave boy who swam across the lake in the path of light from the tower of the Chautauqua building. In a lifetime of retellings, certain phrases had settled into place like keystones:

"curled up in a watermelon rind," "never seen again," and "the path of light"–and the stories developed a lilt and cadence that made Despera Springs seem like a fairy-tale place, not an ordinary town you could find on a map and drive to on an interstate highway.

But here they were, and as far as the eye could see, there was nothing but discount stores, gas stations, used-car lots, and fast-food restaurants.

"We can't sprinkle her ashes here," said Louise. "She'd end up stuck on somebody's shoes and tracked into a nail and tan salon."

Lily was no help. She had just had her heart broken by a banjo player, and all she wanted to do was listen to the Stanley Brothers singing heartache songs and weep.

"Let's go," said Louise. "Just drive around, maybe we'll find a vacant lot, sprinkle her in some weeds, and get on home."

"Oh, your poison love has stained the lifeblood in my heart and soul, and I know my life will never be the same," Ralph Stanley sang from the tape player in a high, keening wail. Lily put the car in reverse, but the tears welled up and she backed smack into the side of a dented-in, scraped-up, painted-over Plymouth Reliant. In a terrible silence they craned their necks and watched the car door creak open and a long leg reach out, agile toes clutching on to blue shower shoes, then the whole man unfolding out of the driver's seat, tall, loose, and lanky.

"We are so sorry, sir," Louise said all in a dither, scrambling out to meet him. "My sister should not be driving a car. She just had her heart broken by a banjo player, and the tears distort her depth perception."

The man stopped and staggered back on his heels. He peered in earnestly at Lily. "Bluegrass?" he said. "Or old-time?"

"Old-time," said Lily.

"Aw, honey, bless your heart." He squatted down and gazed at her sorrowfully.

"Wait a minute," said Louise, rummaging in the glove compartment for the insurance card. "Shouldn't we be examining our cars and assessing the damage?"

"We are assessing the damage," said the man, and he stood up, took two spoons out of his pocket, and went into a little shuffling dance, tapping the spoons high up on his thigh, *chucka chucka chucka,* then down near his knee, hitting the palm of his hand on the upstroke, double time, *ticka ticka ticka.*

"I can't find any dents on your car that aren't already rusted over," called Louise.

With a little flourish he drew the spoons slowly across the inside of his knuckles and slipped them back into his pocket.

"You can trust me," he said to Lily. "I don't play nothing with strings on it."

"Can you help us find something?" said Louise. "We're looking for a lake somewhere around here, where there used to be a building with a tower."

"We're looking for the kind of place where a man might disappear behind a blue mule, or a brave boy might swim in a path of light," said Lily, "to sprinkle our mother's ashes."

"I know what you want," said the spoon player. "Come on." And he shuffled back to his car, the soles of his shower shoes slapping against his heels. Louise punched Ralph Stanley out of the tape player, and Lily drove carefully, with her eyes wide and both hands on the wheel. They followed him out of the parking lot, out onto Highway 90, past a cineplex and an industrial park. His back bumper was crumpled up and hiked up too high on one side, which gave a goofy look to the car, like a dog with one ear wrong-side out. They turned right at a light, then left at a stop sign. They passed a gun and pawn shop and an abandoned scrapyard in a pecan grove. They crossed a railroad track, then the spoon player pulled up into a little alley behind a row of dried-up-looking, old, spindly houses, long ago painted white.

"What are we doing?" said Louise. "Is this safe?"

"Stay on the risers," he said, and they followed him up rotten steps, across a toppling side porch, and out onto the front. There was a little, weedy yard, a crumbling street, then a long slope to a perfectly round lake, shining black in the afternoon sun. Across the lake in the hazy distance they could see an old building with a sagging roof and a crooked octagonal tower.

"Look, Louise," said Lily. "Go get the ashes, it's Despera Springs!"

It was the kind of sight, with the dwindling season, the dappling and the shimmering and the haze, that brings simpleminded emotions to the surface, and Louise stood at the porch railing and thought about their mother, on just such a fall day as this, a happy little girl in this town, now come back for her final rest; and Lily, with the selfishness of the brokenhearted, thought about her lost love, the banjo player, and how she would never be able to stand and look at such a sight with him.

They were both lost in these easy reveries, blinking back cheap tears, when they heard an odd ruffling sound behind them and turned around to see through the screen door an old woman sitting in a straight chair holding an ax in both hands and staring into the fireplace at a big black-and-white Muscovy duck, up to his little gnarly knees in soot and ashes.

"Grab him!" she called out. "Don't let him flap, he'll fling soot all over the house!" The spoon player grabbed the duck with both hands, backed out with him through the screen door, stretched his neck over the porch post, and one two three *whack,* the old woman chopped his head off and he flopped down into the azalea bushes.

Louise sank down on the rotten step and gazed out across the lake with her hands limp in her lap; Lily wheeled around and stared wide-eyed into the gloom of the cluttered room; and the old woman sat down heavily on the top step and grabbed Louise by the knee.

"I am exhausted," the old woman said. "I have congestive heart failure, and any little thing like that will wear me slap out."

It took them different ways. Louise, feeling a maniacal need to establish some kind of order, fell into a patter of formal good manners, introducing herself and giving a brief nonsensical synopsis of their mission here: their long drive, no place for the ashes, the spoon player, the Chautauqua building—"and this is my younger sister, Lily."

But Lily wouldn't stop staring into the house. For some reason, with that whack and flop she had felt the banjo player lifted out of her mind for the first time in months, and images of the cluttered room rushed in to fill the unfamiliar vacancy: clumps of heavy furniture, a crumpled chandelier slouched in a corner like a giant spider, a clothes rack draped with white cotton underwear.

The spoon player finally brought them back to their senses, bouncing around the corner of the house with the duck, picked, drawn, and singed. He rinsed it at the spigot, laid it out in a black skillet, and set it down on the porch beside the old woman, who picked out one last pinfeather.

"They come up from the lake and fly down the chimney," she said to Louise, "and we eat them."

"Oh," gasped Louise. "That makes sense." And she and the old woman settled down quite companionably on the steps with the duck in its skillet and the ashes in their gold-toned urn between them, getting everything straight—"So you are Lila Martin's girls; I had a cousin who married a Martin," the old woman said, and "That was Sid Stringer's monkey, he only loved two things, beer and watermelon," and "Yes, that's the spoon player, he keeps a lightbulb screwed in over at the Chautauqua tower, looks after us somewhat."

Behind them Lily sat on the porch floor, playing with the reflection of the Chautauqua building in her mind. When the breeze died down and the reflection in the lake grew clear and distinct, she could squint her eyes and make herself believe that the reflection was the building itself. This seemed to make anything possible, and she went on to imagine ladies in white lawn and gentlemen in bowler hats strolling in the lake yard, a drunken monkey on a red leash, a blue mule, and a mysterious stranger with a black mustache. Then a little breeze would stir up the ripples, the reflection would slur, and everything would shift back to real. Her mind would clamp down again, and there would be the banjo player on that cold, cold night, nudging her down the walkway and saying, "How could you have thought it was that important?"

"Hey," said the spoon player, looking at her through the spindles. "It's not your fault. You just let love get tangled up in your mind with a stringed instrument, that's all, easiest mistake in the world."

Lily smiled at him, the patient, weary smile of the brokenhearted. "You're sweet," she said.

"I can help you." He wiped his hands on his pants and slid the spoons out of his pocket. "I can teach you to play the spoons." He drew them slowly across his cupped palm with a little muffled cluck. "Hell, I can make you wish you *were* a spoon."

"Let's cook this duck," said the old lady, standing up and tweaking the seat of her skirt straight. "You bring him in," she said to Louise, "I'm not that strong."

"The thing is about spoons is," said the spoon player, "your ears do most of the work."

There was a clatter of pots and pans, rattling and crashing from the kitchen, and a big, sleek rat dashed through the screen door and hurtled off the edge of the porch.

"Sinking ship," said Lily.

The spoon player closed his eyes, screwed up his face, and started singing "Pretty Polly," then came in on the spoons, *chucka chucka chucka*. From the kitchen they heard steady talking, then a frying sound. "I was digging on your grave the best part of last night," sang the spoon player. They smelled cooking onions, garlic, and pepper.

"She's browning it," said Lily. "My sister can cook anything."

"Look here," he said, "you take the spoons back-to-back, you put this finger between here, that gives you your distance."

"But I don't want to learn to play the spoons. I just want to walk down there and look at the water," Lily said.

In the kitchen the clatter settled down and the long, slow cooking began. Louise and the old woman strolled out into the side yard where the early camellias had started to bloom. The spoon player leaned up against the porch post and dozed off with his arms flopped over his bony knees. Lily wandered around the edge of the lake where the ducks were beginning to settle down for the night, standing on first one foot, then the other, tucking their heads under their wings. There was that good pond smell, and the smell of old towns in the fall of the year—piled-up leaves, dry rot, sasanquas, the last of the ginger lilies and the first of the tea olive. Then there was something else—the deep, rich smell of roasting duck.

"There's just enough," said Louise, ladling out dark gravy. Somehow she and the old woman had rummaged out of all that clutter an elegant table setting for four—a white linen tablecloth with a corded monogram, big Blue Willow plates, thin water glasses with chipped gold rims, and in the middle a bowl of sasanquas, pink and ruffly. The whole thing was just beautiful, all blue and white and rosy, and they stood and looked at it for a minute, that peaceful gleaming place smoothed out of all this mess. Then the spoon player said, "I can tell we're gon' eat," and they did.

It was way past dark by the time they had sopped up the last little driblets of gravy, washed the dishes, and flung the duck bones out into the bushes. "Y'all are welcome to spend the night," said the old woman. Then she trailed off down a dark passage, mumbling something about clean sheets.

But there's nothing like cooking and eating the native food of a place to make you feel as if you belong there, and Louise wanted to explore this old town where she now felt so at home. "Let's go walk around the lake," she said. "Bring the flashlight, sir, you can tell us the stories."

There were no streetlights in this left-behind town, and from the edge of the lake they could barely see the houses straggling along the street like the old, dried-up shed skin of a snake. But across the lake one light was shining out of the broken-out windows in the tower of the Chautauqua building.

"Look, Louise," said Lily. "The path of light!" And sure enough, there it was like a wrinkled yellow ribbon stretched out across the black water.

"Well, I'll be," said Louise. "Just like in the story."

The spoon player stepped out and turned to look at Lily. "You could swim across that."

"That's just what I'm fixing to do," said Lily, and she took off her shoes and stepped out of her skirt.

"Lily!" said Louise, grabbing her by both arms and hanging on. "Lily! Something will eat you!" But Lily was already up to her ankles in mud, little pools of water forming around her feet.

"Ain't nothing out there'll eat her," said the spoon player, holding the flashlight up to his forehead and playing the light across the water. "I don't see no red eyes."

"Lily!" said Louise. "You'll drown! Your belly is full of duck!" But Lily was up to her knees, throwing off her shirt.

"That duck will give her strength," said the spoon player.

"Lily!" said Louise. "I'm sure this is against the law!"

"The law ain't looking," said the spoon player.

It felt terrifyingly spooky at first, with the rough grass scratching her legs in the dark and the mud squishing up around her feet. But when she got deep enough to stretch out and swim, she thought nothing had ever felt so good as that silky black water against her skin. At first she swam elegantly, as she had been taught, with long, smooth strokes, lifting her head to the side to breathe. But when she finally stopped to look around, she saw that she had lost the light and was yawing off into the darkness. She treaded water for a minute, twirling around in a panic looking for the light. She couldn't tell whether it was exhaustion or terror making her breathe so hard, deep, gasping gulps and whimpering exhalations, so she just floated for a while to calm down, with her back to the darkness and her face to the starry sky. Then she turned over and began to swim again, dog-paddling with her head up this time, staring straight ahead at the light. How simple it was, she thought, for just this little while—nothing in the world but black water and deep blue sky, and these silly little movements of her hands and feet keeping her alive. Then it seemed as if all at once the light was closer, then quickly closer and closer, then she was in the fringe of grass again, and there was Louise throwing Lily's shirt over her shoulders and saying, "I have never heard of anything so foolish!" and "Lily, what in the world," and there was the spoon player smiling his gap-toothed smile and saying, "I knew you'd come out of it," and they walked back around the street with Lily's teeth chattering the whole way.

They never found the clean sheets, but Louise cleared a space on a sofa in the front room and they fell asleep with their feet propped up on a box fan and their heads on a twelve-pack of toilet paper, Louise still scolding softly, "Why on earth . . . ," and Lily with her hair still dripping, feeling clean and strong, as if with all that gasping and gulping she had finally breathed out something poison that had settled in deep.

It was bright daylight when they woke up. The

spoon player had left in his flop-eared car, and the old woman was rattling around in the kitchen, frying eggs. Lily went out on the porch and looked down at the lake, glittering in the morning sun. Its dark comforts of the night before were gone, and now it looked like something brittle that had shattered into little sparkling chips.

"Look," said Louise, "we forgot all about Mama's ashes." There was the plastic urn still sitting on the top step, with dew beaded up on the gold. They took it down to the edge of the lake, Louise prized off the lid, and without any ceremony she flung the ashes out over the water. A few ducks waddled over, stomped around for a while, then dabbled and rooted around in the mud and shallow water, smacking their bills together, *chucka chucka chucka*—for all the world, thought Lily, like a pair of spoons.

The Green Bus

THERE'S NOTHING hotter than the parking lot of a north-Florida Wal-Mart Superstore in mid-August, but that's where they had been living for over a week when Alice found them and took them home with her—the man, the woman, and the snaggletoothed Chihuahua. They'd been living in their broken-down Volkswagen bus, with a MAKE LOVE NOT WAR sticker on the front and a hand-lettered NEED REPAIRS sign strapped across the back. They had set up two folding aluminum chairs in the shade of a blue FEMA tarp.

They were modern hippies, hippies without a cause from the new millennium; but still it took Alice back—the wild hair, the woman's tie-dyed skirt, the smells of patchouli and sweat, the man's lackadaisical gait.

"Them goddamned slouching hippies," Alice's father had called the hippies in 1967, when Alice had fallen in love with one of them living on a commune behind the old Elmslie place. Roger, with the golden mustache and the dreamy eyes. When they had first moved in with their chickens and their hand plows, her father had thought the hippies were some new kind of earnest farmer, and he gave them an old blue '41 Ford truck he had out back. He spent an afternoon replacing hoses and gaskets, got it running, and gave it to Roger. But the hippies wouldn't use Sevin dust, and flea beetles got their eggplants, and slugs got the lettuces, and possums ate the chickens one by one, and besides, it was the summer of love.

"I gave him my truck, and he took my child!" Alice's father said.

The hippies loved that truck though, and they rode all over in it, hanging out the windows, piled up in the back—Alice, too. It was before the days of seat belts.

"She done took up with them," her father said.

One of the hippies with some carpentry skills built a little house on the back of the truck with a shingled roof and shuttered screen windows, with shelves that folded down from the sides to serve as tables by day and beds by night. In October they all piled in and drove to Washington to march on the Pentagon. They drove all day and all night, taking turns sleeping on the little shelf beds. Roger got beat up and the carpenter got tear-gassed, and Alice heard Norman Mailer make his speech. Then they drove all day and all night back home, dirty and exhausted. They didn't stop at the house, but drove straight to Blue Hole Spring, left the hot truck ticking on the bank, and dropped one by one from the rope swing down into the clear, icy blue.

The truck never ran right after that. It gave its whole heart to the March on Washington. And the commune didn't last either, of course. Roger went to Vermont and joined up with Bernie Sanders and the Liberty Union Party. The carpenter who built the house on the back of the blue truck signed on with Jimmy Carter and Habitat for Humanity. Alice read a startling book called *The Population Bomb,* and when she finished nursing school, she joined the Peace Corps and spent two years in Africa distributing condoms. She got her first real job working at a Planned Parenthood clinic in Houston.

That was all so long ago now, but the new hippies stranded at the Wal-Mart with their Volkswagen bus got Alice to thinking about those long-ago days, the old blue truck, the sunlight dappling the eelgrass in Blue Hole Spring, and the idea she had lost along the way: that things were bad, but people could make them better.

So all that was in her mind when she came out of Wal-Mart with her groceries on a hot summer afternoon and went over to the green bus. "Do y'all need help?" Alice asked. "A cool shower, a home-cooked meal, away from this hot asphalt?" She hadn't really meant to invite them to move in with her, but the next thing she knew, the green bus was parked in her front yard, ticking and smoking just as the old blue truck had ticked and smoked after the March on Washington forty years ago. The new hippies, named Crystal and Jeremy, hauled grocery bags and plastic laundry hampers up onto Alice's front porch, back and forth with their dirty, bare feet.

Crystal had a way of carrying the little dog tight under one arm, mashed up against her bosom, and when she put him down, he still retained that curvature. He sidled up to the corner of the sofa and cocked up a little leg. One side of his lip hung up on a protruding tooth, which gave him a perpetual snarl. His name was Doobie.

"Great porch!" Jeremy called from out back. "This is so cool. You're so nice! We'll just crash here a few days, just until we get money to get the bus fixed, then we'll be back on the road."

Crystal was fat in a comfortable way. She settled down on the sofa in a nest of string bags, draped a crimson-and-purple scarf across her lap, and began to thread beads on a length of hemp twine. She had a series of overlapping rings in the edge of her ear and a gold

morning one of them stood on the back steps and yipped like a coyote. Doors slammed, voices, moist and rhythmic sounds.

"Make love not war," the bumper sticker said. "What would Buddha do?" What *would* Buddha do? Alice wondered as she lay in her bed and watched the dawn. Would Buddha ride up and down the interstate highways in a bus with a fuel leak, being photographed? Would Buddha sit up all night with his fat self on somebody else's sofa, stringing beads? What would Buddha think if he could see the old Elmslie place, where she had all those years ago lived with the hippies and raised chickens and thought she could save the world? Come to find out, she couldn't even save the old Elmslie place. The Big Blue Hole was now a real estate development, ringed with houses and cluttered with boardwalks. It wasn't blue anymore either, but a nasty green, slimy with algae bloom and rock snot. Where the old farmhouse had stood with its falling-off kitchen, the top of the hill had been bulldozed flat and a palacelike house with plastic Palladian windows looked out over a vast lawn mowed in herringbone stripes where the Elmslies had pastured their cows.

At daylight it was finally quiet in the house and Alice put on her scrubs and her crepe-soled shoes. She got a cup of coffee and a bowl of cereal. Doobie came out of the spare room and yapped at her feet, snarling and making vicious little feints at her insteps. He was not used to seeing such big white shoes. But the hippies, "night people," did not stir. Alice got in her car and carefully backed out around the green bus. Through the windshield Buddha sitting in an ashtray on the dashboard looked out at her with a mocking smile.

How far she had come from saving the world! Forty years ago she had been hopefully distributing condoms in desperately overpopulated third-world countries, and now here she was delivering babies to dull-eyed children whose grandmothers weren't thirty years old. "Instant babies," her friend Linda called them.

Her last patient that afternoon was a fifteen-year-old girl in for her first exam at almost full term. Her answer to every question was "Not really."

"Have you made plans? Do you have a place ready for the baby? Do you have financial support? Do you have someone to help at home? Will the father of the baby be any help? Do you know the father of the baby?"

Then it was Wednesday afternoon, the beginning of her three days off. Her feet hurt. Buddha and Krishna and Jesus and all the rest of them have long since washed their hands of us, Alice thought.

When she got home, the side doors of the bus were open and clothes, bedspreads, and blankets were belched out across the lawn and spread over bushes. Jeremy was arranging things on the edge of the porch—a broken plaster-of-paris statue of Adam and Eve was set up on the porch rail, the snake dangling out of a papier-mâché tree with just a few leaves, Eve's hand outstretched for the apple, and Adam broken off at the ankles, lying facedown at her feet like a fallen warrior. In the bathroom, rayon shawls were draped over the towel bar, dripping pools of colored water from their fringes. Crystal had set up a kind of cottage industry in the living room. She had her magnifying lamp set up at the sofa and spools of colored wire, skeins of feathers, balls of string and jars of beads, colored stones and glass, spread out on the table. Finished necklaces hung in the window, and Doobie was yapping furiously, scampering and pouncing on elusive colored spangles that danced across the floor.

"We've decided to have a yard sale," said Crystal, "to raise money for the bus." Alice called in an ad to the paper and the radio station: "Household items, some artwork, jewelry," she said. After supper she pulled out some things from the backs of cupboards and pantry shelves. She would sell her aunt's set of dishes from the 1950s, eight juice glasses with hand-painted flowers, a George Foreman grill. Crystal began gluing rocks together—"A rock from almost every state in the Union," she said. Alice collected boxes and bags and a tin box for change. She wrote YARD SALE, YARD SALE on posterboard with a black marker. She called Frankie from Axelrod's Garage to come look at the bus.

By Saturday morning the front porch looked like a gypsy carnival. The colorful beads hanging along the railing attracted attention from the street, but it wasn't really a hippie-bead kind of town. Alice's aunt's Ballerina dishes went to a young couple with a baby in a stroller. An old lady with diabetes bought the George Foreman grill and the hand-painted glasses from Memphis. The woman next door bought the pretty blue-and-white ginger jar Alice had meant to make into a lamp someday.

Frankie from Axelrod's came by about noon and crawled around under the bus. After a half hour he called Alice over and stood wiping his hands on a greasy rag and glancing with distaste at the engine. It looked pitifully tiny under its little flap. Frankie listed things on his greasy fingers, way up past ten: "Rings, a main bearing, exhaust manifold, fuel pump, fan belt—looks like the oil hasn't been changed in forty thousand miles. Just to get it back on the road, you're looking at three hundred dollars, three-fifty; but to be honest with you, Alice?"

"Don't be honest with me, Frankie," said Alice.

By early afternoon it was too hot for a yard sale.

They took down the signs and counted up the money—$250. "You keep it all," said Alice. "Take the bus to Axelrod's on Monday."

Monday was a nightmare at the hospital. Her coworker Linda had to stay at home with a sick child, a toxemia patient had a seizure, and one of the doctors was tied up in surgery all morning. The little pregnant girl missed her appointment at nine thirty and showed up at two when Alice was busy with an emergency C-section. Alice made arrangements to see her at home after work and fought traffic to get to the other side of town where the girl lived in a beat-up trailer with ragged tuna-fish cans thrown under the steps. They looked like they had both been mangled with the same can opener.

Alice got home late, late. The bus looked different, lighter on its wheels, almost buoyed up. Good old Frankie, Alice thought. The house was empty and quiet. Only Doobie was in the living room, asleep on Crystal's nightgown, which he had scratched up into a little wad. Crystal and Jeremy came in after midnight, Jeremy with his dreadlocks tied up with a scarlet ribbon, Crystal resplendent in a purple-and-coral caftan. They looked elegant in a sloppy way. Crystal flopped down on the sofa.

"Man, that's a long walk!" she said, picking at a blister her flip-flops had rubbed between her toes. She deftly unhooked her bra, extricated it from the armhole of the caftan, and draped it over the lamp. Light glowed through the translucent D cup.

"But the bus," said Alice. "I thought Axelrod—"

"Oh, baby, we got stir-crazy," said Crystal. "I'm not used to being cooped up in a house, so we walked down to the shopping center at the 331 intersection just so I could gaze west down I-10. The highway is in my blood, baby, it's calling me! And there was that fancy Italian restaurant! 'No shoes, no shirt, no service,' it said on the door, but, hey! We were wearing shoes!" She slapped her gold-lamé flip-flop against the fat sole of her foot.

"We had a great meal," said Jeremy.

"With the yard-sale money? You spent your bus money?" said Alice.

"It's just money, baby," said Crystal. "Easy come, easy go."

Under the dual influence of alcohol and complacency they slept soundly that night. The moon glowed on the roof of the bus. It was the yard sale, not Axelrod's Garage, that had lightened its load, Alice realized. She thought about the little pregnant girl twirling a strand of hair around a finger. "Will it hurt?" she had asked. Linda felt as if all the rocks in the United States had been piled on top of her.

Nothing with Strings

From the beginning it was an unusual birth. The girl had come in early in the afternoon. By six she was fully dilated, but the amniotic sac had not ruptured. The contractions were regular and closely spaced, but the girl just lay there. "Push!" Alice said. "It will be over quicker if you push." Her shift ended, but she did not go home. At ten when she checked the girl again, a bulge had formed in the sac, stretched so thin it was transparent. Peering in through that thin, clear membrane, Alice saw a little fist appear and open into a little hand, and then the baby's face floated into view. It was not at all like the first sight she usually had of a baby's face, all squashed and mashed and screwed up from pressure and discomfort. This little face had a wondering look. It seemed to gaze out into the light quizzically, and then retreat, as if to pause and consider. At last the sac ruptured, the water rushed out, and the baby was born all at once.

"Is it over?" the girl asked.

"Almost over now, honey." Alice delivered the placenta, dried the baby off, bundled it in a flannel blanket, and tucked it in at the mother's side. She said what she always said, "You have a healthy baby." But the mother closed her eyes and turned her head away.

Car headlights at night show up flaws in lawn

mowing, and when Alice pulled into her driveway, she noticed a shaggy beard of grass around the bus where she had not been able to reach with the mower. There would be a dead rectangle of grass in the exact shape of a VW bus. She worked efficiently. On her way past the bus, she opened both its double doors on the house side, and starting with the yard-sale leftovers on the porch, she began to load it up, from the back to the front. Adam and Eve went in first. Then the fringed scarves and damp underwear from the bathroom in plastic bags. She packed all the bead-working supplies in a box. She did not try to be quiet, and Jeremy and Crystal came out of the spare room and stood dazed and mute. Jeremy was the first to catch on. He pulled on a T-shirt and then his shoes, hopping on first one foot and then the other.

"I'm sorry," said Alice, scooping up Doobie. "I'm going to need the space."

"But the bus," said Crystal. "We have to get the bus fixed. It won't run."

"It will roll." Alice shoved an armful of quilts into the bus and quickly slammed the double doors before they swelled against them. Jeremy scampered into the passenger side, and Crystal crawled into the driver's seat, still trying to say things. Alice dumped Doobie into Jeremy's lap and slammed the door. There was that good old Volkswagen snap.

"Put it in neutral!" Alice called out, and she got behind the bus and pushed. The yard was level, and it took some doing to get it shoved out of the dents the tires had mashed in the ground and over the raised edge of grass at the street, but there was a gentle slope down toward Miss Gatey's house, and soon it was rolling on its own. At the first intersection Alice heard a *uunnhh-uuhhnn* sound, then a ragged catch and a roar. A belch of smoke drifted up Stegall Street, and the bus was gone.

Alice put her nightgown on, got in her bed, and thought about housecleaning. How she would scrub that spare room! She made a list in her mind of what all she would need: a new string mop, a bottle of Murphy Oil Soap. She wouldn't need that big bed anymore. It was trash day; she would drag the mattress out to the curb. She didn't think about the past or the future. She just thought about that very morning, and how before the sun got on them she would polish the windows in the spare room with newspapers and ammonia.

Almost Gone

"AND NOW I'M going to put in just a liii-ttle bit of cobalt blue right here," said Bob Rigsby, dabbling in his watercolors, and in the angled mirror above his painting table they saw the back of his freckled hand make several little dashes at the paper with the brush, then steady; and then the blue leaked out the tip of the brush, spread across the paper, and soaked gratefully into the oval of rose madder still wet from the last stroke. There was an audible gasp, for there in the mirror, to everyone's amazement, was the side of a rose—the delicate pink of its petal's edge, the shadowed curve, and the pale bulge at the base of the bloom.

Bob Rigsby looked up and stretched his back. He

had a friendly, likable face and a shining bald head, its little feeble hairs now illuminated in the bright light like a glowing halo. "You have to paint what you see, not what you *think* you see," he said, smiling at several of the old ladies on the front row.

From where she stood at the back of the room by the table of sandwiches and lemonade, Della couldn't see their faces, just their feet reflected at the top of the angled mirror. They were the most peaceful feet she had ever seen—no crossing and recrossing of ankles, no shifting to ease an aching hip, no impatient scuffing. They were the feet of happy, attentive listeners. Della smiled. This painting class was by far the most successful of all the cultural events she had put on at the nursing home. There was something mesmerizing about Bob Rigsby—his open face and his gentle lessons in watercolor philosophy and horticultural history.

"This very rose that I am painting today may have been planted by Thomas Jefferson himself at Monticello," he was saying, and he went on with storytelling smoothness to describe the Roundabout Walk, the grove of trees, and the distant mists of the Blue Ridge Mountains. There was the soporific swish-swish of the brush in the water and the little tap-tap against the glass, then a deft stroke, and there went a wavery crimson stripe streaking up through the pink and white.

Suddenly in the middle of all that peace and quiet, old Lila Hardwick yelped, "Monday!"

"Oh, Lila," someone scolded. There was a general grumbling sound, and an impatient scuffle as the contented feet in the mirror shifted irritably.

Bob Rigsby sat up and looked out at them sharply. "Monday?" he said. But the concentration was broken, and people began gathering up canes and walkers. Della announced in her clear, bright voice that it was time for a break. Some people stumped off to the bathroom, some clumped up at the back table for their sandwich and lemonade, and several hung over Bob Rigsby's painting table, peering down at the picture in amazement, as if they could not believe the real thing would look the same as what they had been watching in the mirror.

"How did he make it do that?" said Emily Hancock, and "Now don't it look just like a rose?" said her husband, Harold, and "I have never seen a rose stripedy like that," said Lucille Patterson.

Bob Rigsby was free to have this lunch break to himself in the visitors' lounge or to smoke a cigarette in the Memory Garden, but instead he took his plate and cup into the thick of it and sat right down between old Miss Lila Hardwick and Miss Ethel Livingstone. He handed Lila a cucumber sandwich. "What made you say 'Monday'?" he asked.

Miss Lila didn't say a word, but Miss Ethel Livingstone smacked in exasperation. "I don't know why in the world they keep giving her that Alzheimer's test," she said. "They ask her all these questions, and she never knows anything. She *never* knows what day of the week it is. It's Thursday, Lila!" she shouted, and then said aside to Bob Rigsby, "She doesn't know who the president of the United States is either. She always answers Roosevelt when everyone knows the correct answer is George W. Bush."

Miss Lila munched and munched and munched at a mouthful of sandwich, never taking her eyes off Bob Rigsby's face. It was hard to believe anyone could chew white bread and mayonnaise and thinly sliced cucumbers that long. Finally she swallowed.

"Out by the washhouse," she said.

"There's no such thing as a washhouse anymore, Lila!" snapped Miss Ethel, then she said to Bob Rigsby, "She just wants to think it's still 1933, because she was the queen of the Rose Show in '33."

Miss Lila wore thick glasses slid way down her nose, and her face had shrunk away from her eyes in her old age. It could be disconcerting to be fixed by that magnified gaze, but Bob Rigsby did not waver.

"My mother grew those roses," said Miss Lila.

"What roses?" he asked, leaning closer.

Uh-oh, thought Della. He's apt to get himself into trouble. I'll have to look after him.

◆

Bob Rigsby was a distinguished artist. He was a Dolphin Fellow in the American Watercolor Society, he had been a consultant on the design of the recently issued longleaf-pine postage stamp, and one of his rose paintings, a Mister Lincoln, hung in the White House. Plus, he was just such a nice man.

"What is it that makes people want to feed you?" asked Della.

"All that butter and mayonnaise," said Bob Rigsby. "And look at me! I'm already fat!"

It was the evening after that first session, and partly out of gratitude and partly out of curiosity Della had brought Bob Rigsby supper—the leftover sandwiches, a little salad, and a bottle of wine—and they sat in the front windows of his apartment and looked down on Main Street.

Bob Rigsby lived in an interesting place, the upstairs room over what used to be the old Farmers and Merchants Bank Building downtown. A hundred years ago it had been the office of the bank president, but it had stood empty since the 1930s, and it retained that pleasing stillness of places that have long been abandoned. Through the old, ripply glass of the tall, arched windows and then the lacy leaves of the elm trees shading the sidewalk, they could see the row of handsome brick and granite and cast-iron storefronts across the street with their dates arching in gables and pediments—1882, 1885, 1890.

"Don't you love minds that are almost gone?" said Bob Rigsby. "What fascinating little remnants work their way up out of the clutter of a lifetime of memory—roses and a washhouse."

There was something solid and comforting about the space in that old bank president's office—its elegant proportions, its thick plaster walls, its grand oak wainscoting and rift-pine floor. Della and Bob Rigsby just sat for a while peacefully without talking. The late-afternoon light reflected off the white granite building across the street, so that for just a minute right at dusk, this room was filled with a filmy pink light.

"Everything I love is almost gone," said Bob Rigsby. "Little towns like this, longleaf-pine woods, those old ladies today. Why, even the postage stamp I designed came out just a month before they raised the rates to thirty-seven cents."

They watched the last light slide up the wall, then everything was in shadow.

"Why did she say 'Monday'?" Bob Rigsby mused. "The Rose Queen of '33."

◆

The next day in the art class Bob Rigsby talked about the history of this rose he was painting. "In our young country we know it for its connection with Thomas Jefferson," he said. "But it is a rose of great antiquity, dating from the sixteenth century. It was called Rosamond's rose after Fair Rosamond, an unfortunate mistress of Henry the Second."

In the mirror they saw his wrist twitch, and there was a new fat bud; then his hand slid smoothly across, and what was red on the brush came out a pearly gray on the paper, and there was a shadowed leaf.

Watching it in the mirror gave the whole procedure a once-removed, dreamy feeling, and some of the viewers began talking as if Bob Rigsby weren't sitting right there.

"I heard he painted a postage stamp," said Emily Hancock.

"I have heard that a rose is the hardest of all flowers to paint," said Lucille Patterson, "and look how good he's doing it!"

"Well, of course he can paint a rose, Lucille," said Ethel Livingstone. "He's a famous painter! Just think how many thousands of people have licked that stamp."

"Actually the stamp is self-adhesive," Bob Rigsby said modestly, and he painted on and on, adding a leaflet and a calyx.

"Poor Rosamund," he said, "she didn't last. In one of those long-ago centuries the last syllable of her name got misunderstood as *monde,* the French word for 'world,' and the rose became known as 'rose of the world.'" He rinsed his brush and looked up at them. "I am fascinated by the evolution of rose names."

"Our town is known as the City of Roses," said Miss Ethel, with schoolmarm precision. "Over ten thousand rosebushes are planted in the municipal rose beds."

"Hybrid tea roses and grandifloras," said Bob Rigsby. "There's a bed of Queen Elizabeth outside my window." He peeled up a dried strip of masking fluid, and in the mirror they watched a white stripe appear through the pink and crimson.

"My mother grew those roses," said Miss Lila Hardwick. There was a groan. Once Miss Lila latched on to something, it was hard to get her off it.

"My mother grew those roses," said Miss Lila.

Bob Rigsby stopped and looked up. "What roses?"

"Out by the washhouse," said Miss Lila.

"Lila!" said Miss Ethel impatiently. "We're not talking about out by the washhouse, we're talking about the municipal rose beds downtown. Your mother didn't plant those roses, the city planted those roses in 1995!"

"My mother grew those roses," Lila said.

"Hush, Lila!" snapped Emily Hancock. "Your mother is dead, dead, dead!"

Lila based up and raised her chin. She leaned out and looked down the row at Emily Hancock. "I am the Rose Queen," she said. "Who are you?"

That night when Della brought him supper, Bob Rigsby was so excited he would not sit down, but paced up and down in front of the windows popping cucumber sandwiches into his mouth one after another.

"I spent the afternoon in the newspaper archives at the library," he told Della all in a rush, "and there she was on microfilm—Miss Lila Hardwick, the Rose Queen of '33. Listen to this: 'Over two thousand roses were used to create this rose-covered cart in which rode Morrisville's own Rose Queen, Miss Lila Hardwick, a vision of loveliness well chosen to represent our City of Roses in this third annual Rose Show.'

"It was fabulous!" said Bob Rigsby, wiping mayonnaise off his fingers. "One of the biggest rose exhibitions in the country. They lined the walls of the tobacco warehouse with pine boughs and set up shelves all down the middle for the roses—thousands of roses from all over the Southeast. The streets were strewn with rose petals, the ice company froze roses in huge blocks of ice, there was a grand parade with forty floats and eight bands. And for the Rose Queen they soaked a wicker pony cart in Barnett's Creek overnight and wove the stems of two thousand roses into the wet wicker. They did it every April until the war, and after that they never could muster the enthusiasm for it again, and now seventy years later all they do is plant these pitiful mildewed Queen Elizabeths in the municipal flower beds so they can still call themselves the City of Roses. It's almost gone, but look here. Look at this."

He took out a magnifying glass and a Xerox copy of an old newspaper photograph. There she was, Miss Lila Hardwick, slim and graceful and proud—the Rose Queen of 1933. She had a little held-back smile on her lips, as if she knew more than she was willing to show, and in the angle of her head and the look in her eye there was wit and daring.

"Aw," said Della. "It's all gone."

"Look at the roses she's holding," said Bob Rigsby, playing the magnifying glass up and down over the dim photograph. Della adjusted her gaze away, then closer until she could see—the roses were streaked with wavery dim and dark stripes.

"I would love it so much," said Bob Rigsby, "if that rose she's holding in 1933 is this very rose I'm painting, *Rosa gallica* 'Versicolor,' Fair Rosamund's rose, Rosa Mundi. I would love that so much."

◆

The next day was the last of Bob Rigsby's painting lessons, but instead of holding it as usual at ten in the morning in the recreation room at the nursing home, he invited everyone to his apartment over the old bank building in the late afternoon. "The painting is finished," he told Della. "It will be a kind of unveiling."

It made a lot of work for Della. She had to get enough folding chairs up there and arrange for the van with the wheelchair lift and crank up the old freight elevator at the back of the building to avoid the narrow, rickety stairs in the front.

"I think this is in violation of about eight codes," she said.

"But I need the light," said Bob Rigsby.

It was worrying at first. Della stood up reassuringly in the front of the van and explained over and over. "We are going for a ride to see Bob Rigsby's finished painting unveiled. It's a kind of party or celebration."

But Emily Hancock heard the word *veil* and got the idea that they were going to a wedding, and Lucille Patterson misunderstood Emily and thought they were going to a funeral, and Miss Ethel Livingstone kept busy trying to straighten everyone out.

"Not 'died,' but 'bride,'" she said.

"*Who* died?" asked Miss Emily.

But when they finally got up there and stepped out of the old, creaky freight elevator and onto the second floor, there was Bob Rigsby with his soothing charm, helping them one after another to their chairs like an usher in church. There was the shuffle of settling in, a rattle of walkers, then a general sighing sound as everyone sank down and looked around.

That elegant old room, once so stark and spare, with light as its only ornament, was now filled with color and fragrance. Bob Rigsby had lined the back wall with pine boughs, just like at the grand old Rose Show of 1933, and in front of that greenery he had set up tiered shelves draped in white, each shelf lined with roses in green bottles. They were at the height of their last fall bloom—hybrid tea roses and grandifloras from the municipal flower beds, and from the heritage rose garden in the park blowsy damasks, sweet little China roses, and fragrant Noisettes.

Bob Rigsby let them all just sit for a minute to get their bearings and breathe in the fragrance of cool pine and warm rose. Then he began his last lesson.

"Every rose has a name." He started on the top shelf, holding up each rose and naming it: "Mutabilis, La Reine Victoria, and Mrs. Dudley Cross. Some are named for people. This gold and coral rose Abraham Darby named for a nineteenth-century industrialist; this little sweetheart rose Cecil Brunner named for the daughter of a Swiss nurseryman; this old China rose Louis Philippe named for a French king."

The beautiful colors came and went—the velvety red of a Mister Lincoln, the delicate shell pink of a Souvenir de St. Anns, and the rich gold of a Graham Thomas, as Bob Rigsby named presidents and princesses and distinguished horticulturalists and told their stories: Devoniensis, Céline Forestier, Duchess de Brabant. It was another mesmerizing Bob Rigsby art lesson, and soon nervous hands quit clutching, worried brows unclenched, and under the chairs the feet got still.

As Bob Rigsby came to the last of the roses, that magical reflected light began to gather. "This little pink rose is named La Marne," he said, "and this rose—"

But instead of a rosebud in a green bottle, this time he held up his painting in the last glowing light, that lovely striped rose with its shadowed leaf and its tender bud. Bob Rigsby didn't say a name. He just waited, looking right at Miss Lila Hardwick, the Rose Queen of '33.

"This rose is named . . . ," he prompted, and right then, out of all that clutter of a lifetime of memory, she retrieved it. "The Monday rose!" she screeched.

Bob Rigsby sank down into a chair and mopped his face, worn-out with the exhaustion of effort and accomplishment.

"That is exactly right," he said. "This rose of great antiquity, rarely seen in cultivation today, was known in the twelfth century as Rosamund's rose and is now named Rosa Mundi—or in Lila Hardwick's mother's yard in the thirties where it grew out by the washhouse—the Monday rose."

That night as Della and Bob Rigsby sat in front of the tall, arched windows looking down on the empty streets of that almost-gone little town, every now and then they heard a swish and a flop as the petals of the full-blown roses turned loose of their stems and spilled onto the shelf.

"I love that so much," said Bob Rigsby. "Probably the last thing in her whole life she will get right—the name of a rose."

Acknowledgments

I wish to thank my friends at National Public Radio for their encouragement and generosity through the years.

About the Author

Bailey White was born in Thomasville, Georgia, in 1950, and she still lives in the same house in which she grew up—on one of those large tracts of virgin longleaf pine woods. The daughter of a writer (her father) and a farmer (her mother), White graduated from Florida State University and was a first-grade teacher for many years before devoting herself to writing and gardening full time. She is a regular commentator on NPR's award-winning newsmagazine *All Things Considered,* and she is the author of several books, including the New York Times bestsellers *Mamma Makes Up Her Mind* and *Sleeping at the Starlite Motel.*